COMFORT ZONES

PAMELA DONOGHUE

COMFORT
ZONES

PAMELA DONOGHUE

POLESTAR
BOOK PUBLISHERS

COMFORT ZONES

Polestar Book Publishers acknowledges the support from the publishing programs of the Canada Council, the British Columbia Ministry of Small Business, Tourism and Culture, and the Department of Canadian Heritage.

The artwork on the front cover is "Girl With Shell", used with permission of the artist, Fred Ross, and the owner, Don E. Ring, and with the assistance of the Beaverbrook Art Gallery in Fredericton, New Brunswick.
Cover design by Val Speidel
Editing by Gena Gorrell
Author photograph by Jarvis of Halifax
Printed in Canada

Library of Congress Card Catalog Number: 97-65826

CANADIAN CATALOGUING IN PUBLICATION DATA
Donoghue, Pamela 1962-
        Comfort zones
ISBN 1-896095-24-0
 I. Title.
PS8557.O569C6 1997   C813'.54   C97-910115-8
PR9199.3.D5552C6 1997

in Canada
Polestar Book Publishers
P.O. Box 5238, Station B
Victoria, BC
Canada   V8R 6N4
http://mypage.direct.ca/p/polestar/

in the United States
Polestar Book Publishers
P.O. Box 468
Custer, WA
USA   98240-0468

97 98 99 00 01 5 4 3 2 1

My deepest gratitude and love are extended to the following people:

Carol Bruneau, a wonderful writer, whose support, patience, and wicked sense of humour kept me afloat.

Barbara Jannasch, who allowed me to open, pick up my pen, and embrace all things.

My family, Pat, Meghan, Stephen.

My mother, who never asked me to stop reading, turn off the light, and go to sleep.

My sister Joyce, who bought me books, books, and more books.

Gary, who celebrated my irreverence and sense of the absurd.

My many friends who listened to early drafts of these stories at the beach, over coffee, in washrooms at Christmas parties. You were all a wonderful first audience and the sound of your laughter still rings for me.

I would also like to thank Don McKay, Sabine Campbell, Ellen Seligman and Dick Miller for belief in my early efforts and kind words.

My gratitude to Fred Ross for graciously allowing use of his work, "Girl With Shell." Thank you as well to the owner of the work, Don F. Ring, for his permission, and to Tom Smart, for making it come together.

Gena Gorrell was a tireless and graceful editor, always able to hear what I was trying to say.

— *Pamela Donoghue*

Some of these stories appeared previously in slightly different form: "Lost and Found" and "Last Dance" in *The Fiddlehead*, "The Teller" in *Winner's Circle*, "At One with Nature" in *Pottersfield Portfolio* and *The New Brunswick Reader*, "Comfort Zones" and "Long Distance" in *The Antigonish Review*, "My Soul to Take" in *New Maritimes*.

COMFORT ZONES

for Kathy

COMFORT ZONES

The ice on the sidewalk was patchy, islands with rough edges surrounded by pools of grey slush. When I stepped in the slush, on purpose, it almost reached the silver buckles on my new brown boots. The best thing about new boots was no leaks, no bread bags to put on first. The brim of my blue hat kept sliding down on my forehead, a mass of itching hair, sweat, and damp wool, and I pushed it up, again and again, only to have it fall lower each time.

My nose started running as we walked to the bus stop. I sniffed for a long time but after a while I just let it run, stuck out my tongue and licked my upper lip. The taste was salty and warm, like the gargle I had to do when my tonsils got big.

"Oh God, stop that Lisa," Dan said. He pulled a wadded tissue from his jacket pocket and wiped my nose.

My brother Dan was sixteen. Like a grown-up would, he still made me hold his hand when we crossed the street. His knuckles looked red, his hand so big, but he never pulled me or squeezed my hand too tightly. Stepping off the sidewalk, I could barely see the metal sewers through the ice. In spring I loved to float Popsicle sticks in the streams that formed at the curbs. The sticks would bump along over rocks until they reached the whirlpools and eddies at the big puddles near the sewer. Then the sticks would spin and pause before falling over the edge of the grating and disappearing who knew where.

I wanted to take my hat off but knew Dan would only make me put it on again. You see, the hat had come from Aunt Georgina's throw-away box. We usually got one box in the winter and another in the summer — stuff my aunt had no more use for. Some things were really good, like the white straw purse with only one small tear in the lining, or the pair of shoes for dress-up play with little buttons down the sides. Of course some of the button loops were torn, but I didn't care.

Aunt Georgina's husband died before I was even born. We never talked about that, *long gone* my mother said. Lots of things in the throw-away box would have fit my mother but she just tossed clothes aside, hardly bothering to inspect them.

"Stop," I'd say. "Look at this!"

She'd close her eyes and shake her head, then rub my back and reach for her cigarettes in the pocket of her house-dress.

"Now where would I wear that, sweetie?" she'd ask, and I would try to picture her at the grocery store, pushing a cart well in front of the shiny blue dress, a party dress. When I shrugged she'd continue emptying the box with one hand, smoking with the other, allowing me to grab what I wanted — a pink Kitten sweater, a fur muff with bare spots near the seam. All I'd ever seen my mother keep were blouses, too fancy, so she'd cut off the sleeves and the lacy collars and stitch the edges blunt and plain. My mother and my aunt were not what you'd call close.

My mother had been getting sick for a while, lying on the couch in the afternoons with a facecloth pressed to her forehead. I would bring her a glass of water when I got home from school. She got whiter and whiter, and smaller, until finally she had to go to the hospital for an operation. Gordie, my biggest brother, was gone by then so it was just me and Dan and my father. I guess that's why my aunt decided to invite me for the sleep-over — her way of being nice, figuring I'd be lonely in a house with just men. Maybe she thought I was a bother to care for and wanted to give my father a break, not realizing Dan would be the one taking care of me. My father was my aunt's baby brother. When I was six, she was sixty-two. We always referred to her house as *the big house*.

We called the place we lived a house but it wasn't, not really. It was in the middle of a row of eight units, all of them attached to one another, built after the war. My aunt's house was big compared to our row-house. Plus it was uptown and had huge stone stairs leading to a fancy door with lots of patterned glass. The person answering the door always looked split in pieces through the glass.

Where we lived there were lots of row-houses, one long boulevard running from start to finish, the housing units branching off to each side like a ladder with a line through the middle. Boulevard was a good word to say, rich sounding, so long as you didn't admit everyone there was mostly poor. Mrs. Murphy lived beside us, with her mental-retarded son, Earl. Earl was old, a grown-up, but he liked all the same things I did. He didn't look like the kids in the special class at my school. My mother called it *the opportunity class*. The kids in that class screamed sometimes and the teacher kept the strap on the desk for everyone to see. I knew because my teacher made me take a note over there once and I was scared. My teacher kept the strap in her top desk drawer, and said so long as we were good she would be nice Mrs. Cameron, but if we were bad then mean Mrs. Cameron would come to visit. We were always good. On Valentine's Day she gave each one of us a tiny cinnamon heart when we were lined up to go home. I put mine in the side of my cheek and it felt hot.

Some days after school I went to Mrs. Murphy's and had a snack, toast and milk with Quik. Once she made us a special treat for Earl's birthday, money pancakes, but Earl ate a dime. We think it was a dime because we each had a nickel, a penny, and a dime in our pancake. We found his nickel and his penny. Mrs. Murphy said not to worry, that it would pass. She always used to say not to worry and that was good advice. It made me and Earl feel okay about any mess we made by accident. The clean-up rags were under her sink and I would fetch one, if need be, while Earl smiled at me. Usually Earl and I played crazy-eights until my father came home. If there were no kids around, Earl and I claimed the small patch of dirt at the end of the houses and shot marbles. We both hated the older kids, Earl and I, though it seemed I hated them worse. I hated them with my eyes and my teeth. Earl just used to smile at the ground. He never talked much anyways. Sometimes they yelled at us and once they stole some marbles. I wished Earl could scare them like a real grown-up, but then he wouldn't have been my friend, if he'd been that way.

When my aunt invited me to stay overnight, Dan got ten dollars from Dad and took me to Woolworth's to get new pyjamas. I didn't want new pyjamas but that's what we got — pink flannelette with little giraffes on them. I got a new toothbrush too. Then we went home and Dan made me have a bath.

He ran the water way high in the tub, higher than my mother ever did. Then he told me he'd wait in his room until I was done. I stayed in that bath for a long time, until my fingers were all bumpy like a pair of corduroy pants. Twice Dan knocked on the door and yelled, "You all right in there?" and I yelled, "Yes." There was no need to yell but we did. After I got out and dried off and dressed, Dan came in and washed my hair in the sink. Washing my hair was plain easy because I had a pixie cut. Then we put my pyjamas and other things in a brown paper bag and left to get the bus uptown. When the bus came Dan pulled off my mitten and put the money in my hand, because he knew I liked to drop it in the glass box. There was a little slide inside the box and a trap door — the driver would push a lever and whoosh, all the money would disappear. The seats on the bus were shiny and when we got near the stop Dan let me pull the cord to ring the bell.

I watched television for the rest of the day, my aunt's poodle, Fergus, asleep at my side. Fergus had a skinny red collar decorated with shiny stones and I knew he was an old dog because all he did was sleep. Supper was awful but I ate it, because Dan had told me not to make a fuss. The bread was wrong, not white, and the milk was watery. The carrots were cut funny, little circles. At home, Mom let me eat from her plate. She would cut some of her meat for me and mash her potatoes and carrots into a peach-coloured mountain, then divide it in half with her knife. I would sit beside her, my plate empty except for the white bread with sugar that was my dessert.

After supper, while my aunt washed the dishes, I went into her bedroom and put on my pyjamas. I left my undershirt and underpants on, something I never did at home. It seemed less permanent, my being there, that way.

I watched more television until my aunt came into the living-room, in a dark paisley dressing-gown.

"Washroom time," she said.

We called it the toilet at home. *I need to go to the toilet. Is anyone in the toilet?* Sometimes Dan laughed at that and said, "Who's in the toilet?"

My aunt brushed her teeth and I brushed mine, mostly chewing on the bristles with my back teeth, sucking and swallowing the sweetish, minty foam. She kept the water running the whole time. Then she took a white facecloth from the shelf beside the sink and held it under the hot-water tap until it was wet. When she had wrung it out and folded it, she passed it to me, nodding downward. I looked up at her and she nodded downward again, a small frown between her eyebrows.

"Wash now," she said.

I paused. Wash … wash what?

She must have seen my confusion.

"First your front passage, then the back passage," she said.

The back passage was a hidden path Earl and I had made where the row-housing ended, between an overgrown white lilac tree and a high wooden fence. What was the front passage? And then she pointed, looking flustered, to my pyjama bottoms.

I knew what she meant: she wanted me to wash my bum. What was all this about passages? Besides, couldn't she tell I had been in the tub that very morning? I felt embarrassed, and I didn't want the now cold facecloth making me wet and clammy against my new pyjamas. My aunt must've figured I was shy because she turned and looked the other way. Pulling open the elastic waist of my pyjama bottoms, I was able to bypass my underpants with the facecloth, only washing the top of my leg. After what felt like a long time, my aunt turned to face me again.

She opened the laundry-chute door, a little hinged thing beside the sink, and pointed. I threw the cloth down the hole and the door snapped shut.

I lay very still in the four-poster bed. It was the highest bed I'd ever seen, kind of like the princess-and-the-pea bed. My aunt had her back to me and made a soft clicking sound when she breathed. At first I feared she was going to make me sleep in my dead uncle's room, the one with the giant bullet made into a table lamp. I mentioned how at sleepovers the people have to sleep together, that's the whole fun. While I told her this I walked to her room and put my bag on the floor beside her big dark wardrobe. I thought of all the nights Mom came into my bed and slept close beside me, her breath soft and warm on my hair, the blankets tangled around us. Mom was like the capital letter S, she said, and I was like the small letter s, and that was why we fit so nicely together. My aunt would never hug or cuddle me. She had never even kissed me; instead she kissed the air near my face.

The tears came suddenly, quiet little rivers softening the stiff white pillow-case. I was lying on my side, so the tears from my top eye had to run over my nose and fall off. The other eye leaked directly onto the cold cotton. I cried with no sound for as long as I could. Then I turned on my back and sniffed, a huge sniff, sucking in the tears and mess from my nose.

My aunt awoke. She sat up and turned on the bedside lamp, looking down at me, her grey hair loose and fuzzy.

"Good lord," she said, scratching her ear.

She opened the drawer of the bedside table and pulled out a white lacy handkerchief. I quickly wiped my nose on my sleeve. When she handed the handkerchief to me I gently dabbed my lips and passed it back to her.

"Did you have a nightmare?" she asked.

I shook my head.

"Pain in your abdomen?"

I shook my head again.

"Well what is it then?"

"I'm lonely," I said. "I'm lonely is all it is."

I said it twice so she would know it to be true. Times she seemed a little deaf and my voice was all shaky from crying. She groped for her slippers and pushed aside the blankets. I shimmied to the edge of the bed, slid to the cold floor and heard Fergus's nails clicking on the wooden floor of the hall-way.

I sat at the kitchen table while she fussed in her pantry, light shining out into the dim night kitchen. I was thinking she must wish she could put me in the throw-away box. I had held in my sobs for so long that now my breathing turned into the shudders.

My aunt put four digestive biscuits on a small pink plate, but as soon as she set it on the table the phone rang. She jumped a little and grabbed the black receiver by the fridge.

"Hello," she said, sounding frantic. "Oh Dan. Well, it is rather late … Back on the ward is she … Fine. Yes, I'll tell her … No, not asleep … I think she was but she woke up, a little lonely … My lord, it's half-past ten, young man … No … Yes … All right, I'll have her ready."

She turned to me with a funny look on her face, between sad and mad but more sad.

"That was your brother. He said your mother is fine, the operation went well. He'll be here in ten minutes to take you home. Seems to think you may be a little young for this after all. Come on and we'll pack your clothes."

I was allowed to wear my pyjamas home, my green jacket over top. We sat on the hall butler, the cloudy mirror behind us and curly hat-hooks up and down the sides. On other visits we'd heard about the rescue of the hall butler from the Great Fire by some long gone relative. When the car headlights came and stopped in front of the house I stood up and hugged my aunt. She gasped a little but then she leaned forward and hugged me back, a hard, tight hug, like Mrs. Murphy gives me at Christmas-time.

I got to sit in front, between Dan and his friend Mark. Mark drove because it was his car. He had blond wavy hair and wore a high-school jacket. Dan kept picking at his jeans and singing along with the radio. I felt happy, and sniffed in the comforting smell of cigarettes, of old car and oil.

Dan tucked me into bed when we got home, told me him and Mark were going to play a few hands of cards. He said Mom would be staying in the hospital for a few days but that he had talked to her and she sent me all her love. I hoped she had nice women in her room and tried to picture them all drinking tea and laughing. For a while I listened to them in the kitchen, the sound of the fridge opening, someone dialling the phone. Then I wrapped the blankets around my legs and watched the streetlight through the window until I fell asleep.

THE TELLER

"Never look a gift horse in the mouth."

Jocelyn's mother, Georgina, delivered this piece of wisdom with the same knowing, clipped voice she used for all her advice. Jocelyn's mother was never short of advice, predictions of ill health or tight, self-righteous smiles. Because her frequent forecasts of bad fate at one time or another proved accurate, she felt herself in connection with the power that doles out misfortune to those who deserve it.

Jocelyn never knew why she shouldn't look in the mouth of the gift horse. She had a vague notion of hidden soldiers, bows and arrows, big wooden wheels and armed guards at a gate; but it seemed part of some hazy dream. She wondered whether her mother knew the real story behind the phrase, or any of the hundreds of others she lived her life by: a watched pot never boils; a stitch in time saves nine; joy in the morning is grief in the evening. Then, abruptly, her mother died. Jocelyn imagined the shocked face, the hand clutched to her traitorous heart, as she croaked out the words "one crow sorrow ..." before she fell to the gleaming hardwood floor with a decisive thud.

I miss my mother. Strange, but now that she's dead I realize how much I missed her the whole time she was alive. This may sound crazy, but I miss her less now and on good days I feel she can truly hear and understand me. All the surprises of life, the surprise realizations, come to me like this — the same way we used to sneak up behind each other as kids and karate-chop the victim behind the knees, causing her to bend and fall forward with a gasp.

Jocelyn has two children, both boys, aged ten months and four years. On Wednesday mornings she attends a mother-and-tot playgroup at the YWCA. She used to go to exercise classes but she missed a month when, one after the other, both boys and her husband all had chicken-pox. After that she quit exercise, and recently she has started smoking again — secretly. Buying the little fifteen-packs of ciga-rettes, she smokes in the bathroom, usually while "Sesame Street" is on and the baby is napping. With the exhaust fan on, she sits on the floor, back propped against the door, flip-ping through the Sears catalogue or sometimes Canadian Living.

Jocelyn's husband, David, is a chartered accountant; they met six years ago, attending university in Toronto. David is from Waterloo, Jocelyn from the Maritimes. After gradu-ation Jocelyn secured a fine entry position with a public relations firm. David, still mired in books, claimed to be proud and excited but in fact felt envious, and told him-

self that she had got the job because they had a mandate to hire more women. Two months later, when they discovered that Jocelyn's diaphragm had slipped, they sat on their new striped Ikea couch discussing options. Jocelyn wanted an abortion and was surprised at David's insistence that they have the baby. She gave in with little struggle and David was incredibly attentive and helpful throughout the pregnancy. Six months after the baby was born, David received a job offer in Halifax. They moved before Jocelyn returned to work from maternity leave. She stayed home with the baby after the move, largely because she couldn't find a competent babysitter. She and David planned the second pregnancy, both feeling the life of an only child to be a sad and lonely existence, based on Jocelyn's experience.

You probably think all this "I'm a little teapot" stuff is some indication that I'm half brain-dead. You probably don't know the actions for "Miss Polly had a dolly" or "Itsy-bitsy spider". I want to tell you something — I wasn't always like this, bits of chewed banana rubbed into the sleeve of my sweater, legs sporting two weeks' growth of stubble. Unless you have more compassion than I give you credit for — and I'm a great judge of character — I suggest you lower your Ray-Bans and listen to me for a while. As my grade ten math teacher used to say, "You might even learn something." He wore a gold chain around his neck with a pendant proclaiming him #1. The top three buttons of his shirts were never fastened and the pendant danced about on his pale, hairless chest, the skin like flaky pie-crust. The shirt buttons pulled across his bulging stomach, so fat it hid the buckle of his belt. I used to wonder whether the pendant had anything to do with math. Was it from his wife? Did he have one? What was she like? Was it from a secret lover? Unfortunately, I learned less than I should have that year in math.

I like my life and I love my husband. I bet you're thinking that I'm some kind of doormat, that love melted me into some slush puddle of subservience. The Inuit have a slew of words for snow, depending on what kind of snow it is, and we have this one word, love, which we toss around with the degree of care usually reserved for flinging confetti. I love pizza, I love the movie "Butch Cassidy and the Sundance Kid", I love Leonard Cohen. Okay, let's get a little more specific. By love I mean respect, and for us the feeling is mutual. That's why I can do this stuff with some ease. I mean, I value the role of caregiver for the children but it's inevitable that I end up doing the big share of mindless chores.

I've cut way back on the housework, not that I ever threw myself into it with any gusto. I paint with the kids, read, play with little cars and tiny plastic people that have no legs. I haven't figured out why they made them that way. The dog and the sheep have legs. Oh well, I'm sure there's a reason. The people fit in the cars and the animals don't.

My kids will remember me singing and twisting to Raffi, not wearing rubber gloves and hanging my face in the toilet or, worse, crawling into the oven to scrub off the black stuff with all those carcinogenic cleaners.

Perhaps you think my self-care has gone down the tubes. I've quit four of the five steps in the Mary Kay skin-care program. I wear dark-coloured track suits that don't show the dirt, and on the authenticity scale I rank way up there. I'm living my own life and I think my value lies not in being nice and good but rather in being honest and sincere. I never say yes when I mean no and I've never bought a self-help book. I mean, if you can't help yourself, all you help is those slick writers who end up with a time-share condo in the Bahamas by preying on the weak and suggestible in our society. I think Oprah and Phil do a lot more damage than they do good.

Jocelyn does her banking on Wednesdays, after playgroup. She puts the baby in a backpack carrier and squeezes her toddler into the stroller, only because he's tired at that time of day. By rushing, she manages to arrive at the bank before lunch, when the lineups aren't long.

This particular Wednesday has not gone well. The baby fell off the elephant slide at playgroup and has a nasty bump on his chin. The toddler got soaked at the water-play table and is whining about his wet shirt. The parking meters near the bank were taken and she had to park in a lot down the street.

She chooses not to use the instant banking machines in the foyer because she distrusts machinery, dislikes automation. As she waits in the lineup she sorts her papers and doles out crackers to the children. The baby sucks his and rubs pieces into her hair and collar.

The green arrow flashes; she carefully manoeuvres herself and the stroller to the open wicket, puts her papers on the counter. Only then does she look up to see the teller. His face appears very open, and his eyes are brown, so attentive. This is how she will later think of him. For a moment she forgets the weight of the baby on her back, the sounds of the child near her feet, and smiles at the teller, so young, so new he seems to shine. He smiles back — white, even, banker's teeth — and starts to carry out her transactions. She is buying a money order in British currency for her mother-in-law's birthday. He keeps smiling, enthusiasm coupled with innocence, not rushing at all, and he leans over the counter to whisper to her.

"Are you interested in foreign currency?" he asked.

I wasn't sure what he was asking me so I got him to repeat it. He was leaning over the counter towards me, kind of whispering in a "let's-share-a-secret" voice. I whispered "yes" with a lot of enthusiasm, although I know absolutely dick-all about foreign money and don't have much interest in our own. I guess I just wanted to go along with the mood … smug, happy conspiracy.

He reached down under the counter, retrieved an envelope and proceeded to tell me that he collected foreign money, had a friend at the main branch — where all the foreign stuff gets sorted or something — who saved it for him to buy. He said that most people didn't appreciate the hobby, the genuine beauty of the foreign notes. Honest to God, that's what he said, *genuine beauty of the foreign notes*. He passed me one after another, not even checking to see if my hands were clean, and showed me how to see the watermarks by holding the bills up to the light. The countries kept coming and coming, Spain, Holland, Turkey, Egypt.

We looked at them together and he continued to talk to me, softly, with a breathless excitement. He seemed quite lovely, as fresh as the new bills he held out for inspection. Finally the baby gave my hair an especially hard yank and jolted us all back into this country. Sliding everything into the envelope, he put it under the counter, filled out my money order, made my deposit and cash withdrawal. He waved at me as I left, and I waved back with a hand full of cracker pieces.

The next week Jocelyn had a different teller, a middle-aged woman, stout and heavily made up, who tried to sell her a cookbook to support the local children's hospital. Jocelyn de-

clined the offer of the cookbook and, trying not to be obvious, swept her eyes over the line of tellers in search of the young man. He was there; he looked up to see her and waved wistfully. Or so she thought.

The week after that she had yet another teller but the young man saw her and smiled down the row of bent heads scribbling signatures.

I am not a vain person. I realized long ago that my most attractive feature to men is my ears. Well, not my actual ears. It's just that I listen. I really do, because for the most part I care and I'm interested enough to pay attention. One of my girlfriends says I'm approachable, she doesn't mean easy, and the word fits in some ways. It's something to do with my looking relatively happy and content, as if I would be fun to curl up beside with a good book. David and I used to spend all of our Saturday mornings in bed, a thermos of black coffee on the floor and itchy toast crumbs falling into bed with us. We had a navy and ecru cover for the goose-down duvet, our first mutual purchase. We read three newspapers David bought from the tiny corner store, and his kisses tasted of Seville orange marmalade. This was all before children.

I say I'm not vain because it embarrasses me to tell you this next part. I don't usually check my bankbook when it's handed back to me, but last week I looked and my balance was a lot bigger than I expected. After I got home and settled the kids in front of the television with banana slices and a new video from the library, I sat down and pulled out the bankbook to look more closely. There were two five-hundred-dollar deposits to my account that I had not made. Looking at the dates in the book, I checked my wall calendar. The first deposit had gone in on Thursday, two weeks ago, and the other one last Thursday. I called David at work but he was no help.

Well, I guess you realize I suspect the teller at the bank. Yeah, I really do think it's him putting this money in my account. I don't think it's his money, either. I think he's pulling it from some account where it'll never be noticed and putting it into mine. You know, a lot of things are possible now that everything is computerized; computer theft or fraud, whatever, is rampant. Things are not all so safe and secure as they would have you believe.

So that's it. I'm going into the bathroom for a smoke. This time I'm leaving the fan off because it drives me nuts. I wonder if he has a girlfriend. He's the kind of person I wish attracted me but I'm hopelessly drawn to the so-called strong men. I'm smiling like some kind of fool but I have to do something. I just don't know what.

The following Wednesday Jocelyn enters the bank with the firm intention of doing nothing at all. She can hear her mother's voice as if from a great distance — what comes around goes around; never look a gift horse, never look a gift horse — so Jocelyn begins to hum softly to herself, the tune filling her mind. She is nervous and excited. She looks up and down the row of tellers but he isn't there. She goes home and reads the newspaper, sitting in the car in the driveway because both children have fallen asleep during the drive home.

> *From the* Mail Star, *February 22, 1993:*
> Michael Evans was arrested and charged yesterday with four counts of reckless endangerment after he was revealed to have

used a bizarre method for meeting women — shooting out their tires with a pistol.

Evans, a 22-year-old bank teller, periodically drove along a twenty-kilometre stretch of highway between Halifax and Peggy's Cove, on the lookout for attractive women, he told police. On at least six occasions, Evans manoeuvred his pickup truck behind a vehicle driven by a woman and shot the victim's left rear tire with a .22 calibre pistol. When the victims pulled over, Evans stopped to help, offering to change the tires and drive the women to nearby service stations or to their homes.

"He actually drove two of the women to their homes and had coffee after their tire blowouts. They said he was one of the nicest guys they'd ever met," reported RCMP constable Stephen Darley.

Evans pleaded guilty to all four counts and will reappear in court on March 17th for sentencing.

LOST AND FOUND

The year I was in fourth grade, I found Jesus not once but twice. That was also the year Mr. Rideout christened me, Lisa, a "smart cookie" and I got my first pair of glasses. We left my father in October so I changed schools. He drank and raved — that's what we called it, raving … he was raving. I used to sit behind the old burgundy wing-chair, staring at the ribbed fabric, my fingers jammed in my ears. Periodically I'd ease my fingers out to check if the raving was slowing down. Then I'd shove them back in. Eventually a gentle roar like the sea would fill my head, I'd forget about my fingers in my ears and, by the time I finally removed them, he'd have gone up to bed to sleep it off.

Everyone at my new school was Catholic. Bridget, Angela, Scott and Darlene. I guess they just figured I was Catholic too, and I was happy to let it go at that. My Anglican upbringing had been slipshod at best, consisting mainly of new knee-socks, a white straw hat, white cotton gloves and black patent-leather shoes at Easter. We didn't do God at Christmas, only Easter. The only hymn I recall is "Christ the Lord Is Risen Today", warbled by our neighbour, Mrs. Lyndon, a determined soprano who no doubt had God jamming his fingers in his ears.

Every Wednesday we met in the basement of the church for catechism. Sister Mary Theresa took a shine to me; by all appearances I was a good listener, leaning forward in my seat and nodding a lot, an eager pupil. The first week we practised genuflecting, down on one knee, eyes on the pyx. My movement was fluid, reverent, submissive, down and then effortlessly up and into the pew. Sister Mary Theresa made everyone watch me and I did it five times, perfectly. By the time the next week arrived I'd mastered the Hail Mary, the Catholics' stopped-short version of Our Father, the Apostles' Creed and the Nicene Creed. I recited them for the group, Angela absently picking a scab off her knee, Scott wiping his nose on his sleeve, and afterwards Sister Mary Theresa squeezed my shoulder and beamed beatifically. She gave me a rosary for my birthday and every day after school I would climb the steep hill to church, pull open the huge, dark brown door and step inside. My favourite moment was the instant of the door whispering solid shut behind me while my eyes adjusted to the cool gloom of the vestibule. I'd dip my fingers into the damp concrete pool of holy water, bless myself and go inside.

Usually I lit a candle first, just to get things going. One or two old women would be knelt in prayer in a back pew, frozen in silence, as good as dead. I'd drop my quarter, saved from recess money, into the tin box and listen to the gentle clink as it nestled amid its kind. The wooden sticks stood soldier-like, feet implanted in the sand, and I always picked the longest one, caught the flame from a glowing candle and lit a new one, kneeling on the purple-carpeted step to pray. Some days I did my rosary and other days the Stations of the Cross. I'd make sure I arrived home fifteen minutes before my mother got off work at the switchboard, where she got me bundles of blank, coloured notepaper, the kind she wrote her messages on.

In February my uncle got in the tub with the toaster. Anyway, that's as much as I could figure from my mother's whispered phone conversations. Oh, and that he was crazy, of course. We took the train to Montreal to visit him. The train wasn't the best part, nor was eating chocolates while we sat beside my pale uncle propped in the hospital bed in a yellow nightgown. The best part was the visit to St. Joseph's Oratory. I found it quite by accident, out walking with my sixteen-year-old cousin and her boyfriend. They weren't too happy to be walking me, but they enjoyed the chance to kiss and grope at each stoplight, safe from the scrutiny of my bony-fingered aunt.

Sister Mary Theresa had mentioned St. Joseph's Oratory to me when I'd told her I was going to Montreal. We turned a corner and there it was. My heart was pounding and I asked if we could visit. My cousin gave me a dollar, told me to visit it myself and said she'd meet me at the same spot in one hour. I couldn't believe my good fortune, watching them run away holding hands. My first stop was the gift shop. I read a brochure — a prayer while kneeling on every step from bottom to top of that infinite staircase, and the promise of a miracle. Time was not on my side. I grabbed a bottle of holy water, eighty-nine cents, stuck the change in the pocket of my parka and ran to the steps. Hail Mary seemed the wisest choice, short and snappy. I got right to business and by the tenth step I was silently reciting it quickly enough to sound like someone on the radio, talking smoothly and really fast.

I prayed that my father would go to heaven when he died. I knew he didn't believe in God at all. It was one of his favourite topics, the stupidity of those "mickey Liberal bastards". He always yelled it as if it were one word, "mickeyliberal-bastards", and for many years I thought it was one word and I was Christly happy not to be one because they sounded godawful.

By the time I reached the top of the stairs, my fingers were stiff and my nose and eyes running with the cold. I checked my watch and raced back to the gift store, five minutes left. For a mere dime I purchased a postcard depicting the steps on a sunnier day.

By the next Saturday we'd caught the train back and were at Deluxe French Fries with my father. He visited us every Saturday morning, bringing his laundry. My mother would hand him a bag of clothes from the previous week, now cleaned and ironed. We drove out for lunch, the three of us, the visit being to provide me with some quality family time. My parents barely spoke, my mother chain-smoking and drinking coffee, my father spearing his fries on a weak wooden two-pronged fork and me dipping mine in a semi-solid pool of pale gravy. Raving being my father's prime mode of communication, he was relatively quiet on these trips, and when the fries were gone he drove us home. Before we got out of the car I always kissed his cheek, smooth and firm. This week I showed him the postcard.

"What's this?" he asked gruffly.

I cautiously hurried to explain. "It's a place where people pray on every single step and if they get to the top they believe their prayer will be answered."

"What kind of Christly moron would do a thing like that?" he bellowed. "Stupid goddamned mickeys."

I stuffed the postcard in my pocket and got out of the car, secure in the knowledge that his fate was sealed, safe behind those pearly gates, and that God would overlook his future outbursts.

Spring came, as always, water gushing to the sewers and the ditches smelling of something vaguely sour. I walked to school quickly, anxious to show off my new marble-bag from my cousin. She was at university in Fredericton and the bag had come in the mail, brown tweed lined with beige satin and a dark brown shoestring for a tie. The black church Chevrolet pulled up to the curb and Sister Mary Theresa motioned me over. I ran up and she rolled down the passenger window to speak to me. She told me that I must stop receiving Holy Communion as she'd found out I was not a Catholic, and that it would be best if I stayed away from the church. I lost God, four pretties and six glassies that morning.

When school finished in June we moved back in with my father. My room was exactly as I'd left it, not an item moved. He pulled sheets of plastic off everything — he'd covered it to keep the dust off. My mother decided to send me to camp for eight days and seven nights. We shopped for pyjamas, toothpaste and soap, and as a present my mother bought me a box of rainbow-coloured writing paper and a retractable ballpoint pen. Next thing I knew I was travelling on the camp bus, Rock of Ages, with thirty other kids aged eight to twelve.

The camp's theme was decidedly rustic: no running water, ripped screens. We ate in the huge hall on hard benches at long wooden tables, cold cereal, cold macaroni and cheese and finally cold mashed potatoes and meat. I couldn't understand how the food could get so cold when everything else — my lumpy cot, my clothes, my head, the arts and crafts supplies — felt steaming hot. We went in the river once a day. My soap didn't suds but I rubbed myself with it to get the dirt out of my scratched-raw mosquito bites. I gave up on my teeth.

We did crafts in the morning and afternoon, all with a religious theme. We made crosses from toothpicks, Popsicle sticks and birch branches. We wrote "Jesus Loves You" on rocks in yellow poster paint. After the evening meal the tables were pushed against one wall and we sat on the benches and sang. "This little light of mine" and "One way God said to get to heaven, Jesus is the only way". The guitarist was a bald elderly man who owned a shoe store at the top of King Street. He wore a toupee to sell shoes but not to camp, I wasn't sure why. His head glistening, he laid the guitar down and stood to pray. We all fell to our knees on the rough wooden floor. He started slowly but the tempo grew and grew, until after a time he was raving. I couldn't believe he was drunk and couldn't understand how anyone could rave sober. He raved of hell and sin, damnation and burning fires, evil, more damnation, and I didn't dare plug my ears. Finally, when he could rave no more, his wife came to the front and he collapsed heavily onto a creaking wooden folding chair. She had lots of hair, blonde and in a bouffant of sorts, a beehive affair that reeked of Dippity-do and Breck hairspray. Her voice was soft vanilla ice-cream and she told us that all we had to do was get reborn in Christ. It sounded easy enough, too easy. I had my doubts. But she said that if we came down front and accepted Jesus as our personal saviour our names would be written in his book for ever and we would be saved. I wondered about erasers, that's the kind of person I was at that point. A few kids went down, girls mostly, and as they knelt she put her hands on their heads and wept. I figured I'd hold off for a few days.

The shoe-store man stood up and made his way to the back of the hall. His eyes were shiny now, like his head; they weren't the eyes that looked at me when he pressed the toes of my blue leather Buster Browns to see if they fit all right. He'd barely made it halfway back when he fell to the floor. We all turned. He started writhing and yelling in a strange garble and his wife sang out, "Praise the Lord, the gift of tongues." I knew people could swallow their tongues or bite them off in a fit and I figured this was a fit. I'd seen one before — Angela's older brother started fits after he fell off his bike one summer. He had a fit right in Manchester's, the fancy big department store uptown! But I didn't remember him yelling this stuff, kind of a mix of pig Latin and baby talk. No one seemed too worried, but then I was the new-comer — the other kids all went to the same church every Sunday and got treated to this each week, I expected. All I knew was that I wanted to put some distance between me and the gift of tongues, so I made my way up to the front, and got clapped on the head and enveloped in a sea of tears and hairspray.

"Praise Jesus and what is your name, child?"

"Lisa," I mumbled.

"Lisa, let's kneel in prayer. Your name is now written in the Lord's book, Jesus' book, you are saved and reborn. Praise Jesus' name. Amen."

My mother came to get me the following Saturday. My father drove. They seemed happy and I knew we wouldn't be eating french fries at Deluxe for a while, anyways. I fell asleep in the bathtub when we got home. My friend Rachel came to get me later and we went to our secret rock, the airplane rock, named for its shape. We ate red liquorice and traded comics. When it got dark we started walking home. From everything I'd heard at camp hell was very bright, like a giant bonfire mixed with red and yellow fireworks. But I couldn't help wondering if maybe they had gotten it wrong, that hell was actually dark — that hell was more like the drainpipes under the roads — full of plain old dirt and cold muddy water.

LONG DISTANCE

The only person I want to talk to is Evan, but of course Evan is dead. Oh, I know it's all fine and well to talk to dead people these days, but it's not something I'm comfortable with. I teach grade nine English and history. This morning I read aloud from *Jonathan Livingston Seagull* and later, having a smoke in the teachers' lounge, I noticed my hands were shaking.

One of the girls in my home-room class, Lisa, is sending me notes. She's a strange girl, a loner, incredibly bright. Her mismatched combination of features should make her homely but results in an unexpected beauty. Once every few years a student has a crush on me. I'm not attractive so it's never the usual girls — the ones who laugh about boys, draw little happy faces underneath their names, paint their finger-nails shades the colour of the lupins that grow in the field behind the school — who titter over me while they get books from their lockers. They would be so much easier to deal with. I hide the poems Lisa writes me in an antique gin-ger-beer crock on the mantel at home.

Dear Mr. Garrod,

Thanks for reading to us every day. It's my favourite part of the day. I bought the book and read it myself but it's better to hear you reading out loud. Don't worry about the jocks at the back who aren't listening. They never listen to anything important.

You are a very good teacher. I know it's not cool to like school but I do, like it that is. Ever since first grade I've liked it. All except home ec because I'm trying to sew a terrycloth bathrobe thing that keeps jamming in the machine. We're having this stupid dinner for the teachers next week and we'll be serving you food. Don't sit at the table I'm serving because it's too embarrassing and we have to wear white aprons like waitresses and the food will probably be cold by the time you get it. Would you please save these two poems I wrote somewhere safe? If you can't, that's okay, just give them back to me and please don't show them to anyone.

Lisa, class of 9G

You sit in silence, without peace
Fold your worry hands
War of the Roses, Jonathan,
Maps of vanished lands.
If I cried, and can't, won't, wouldn't
There would not be enough red plastic buckets
Sand-covered beach toys
Castles falling over with the tide
To bail the tears.

&

Sign in the emergency department
"Not responsible for valuables left in this
   department"
I'm wondering if they mean lives.
Sad yellow walls, wrinkled and split,
Dirty windows, can't get out, can't get in.
Down the hall somewhere they splint fix
My friend's ankle, twisted but broken too.
There are dead people in the basement here,
Broken, return to sender, defective, warranty
   expired.
An old, old woman, the oldest ever,
Digging in her purse, a Kleenex falling from her
   sleeve,
Stops to pick her ear and frown at me.
Feel like a lost bird, flying into windows
Feathers bloodied, heart pounding under wing —

My neighbour crushed a pigeon on the road
Wounded, couldn't fly
He found a huge rock and killed the bird.
Said that was the decent thing to do.

We don't mention Evan now, except in a roundabout way. Every year about this time my mother calls me, long distance, and says, "Brian, next week is May ninth you know." Then she proceeds to prattle on about the neighbours, how the paperboy always lets the aluminum door slam, the mechanic at Canadian Tire who broke his wrist last time she was there. She talks, one topic fusing with the next, and I listen. Her endings are always the same: "My love to Dolores and the children."

The purpose of her call is to remind me to put a memorial in the newspaper back home. On the anniversary of Evan's death my mother and her sister place an ad, and it's expected of me to do the same. Do they think Evan takes the paper now? I would never hurt my mother — it's simply something my family does, this memorial stuff.

Dolores will handle all the details, call the newspaper and choose the stock verse, give them our credit card number. Dolores understands my mother but so far has never been able to explain her to me. My mother always puts Evan's high school graduation photograph at the top of her notice. Dolores told me. I never read them. Not once, in the eight years since his death.

I know Evan's suicide was not impulsive, not because of a transitory sadness. I know because I found him. Dad's retired and our parents had gone to Florida for three months. Evan was a freshman at the local university, still living at home. I was born quite late in their marriage and then, fifteen years after me, they had Evan. No one could believe it, least of all them. What with their age, Evan's birth was kind of a scandal, in a town and a time when scandals were hard to come by.

My trip to our home town was unexpected — I had to fill in for our department head at a Provincial meeting. When I tried to call Evan there was no answer so I figured he was studying or at a night class. I drove over later, after all my meetings were done. The doors were locked and the house was dark. I'm not sure why but I looked in the garage. Dad's car, a Chrysler Fifth Avenue, was there and I could see Evan's body in the back seat.

The police found me just by chance. Our house is a bit outside the city and on a large lot. They saw my car with the lights on while they were doing a routine patrol and came to investigate. I had wrapped Evan in the grey army blanket that Mom kept on the back seat and I was holding him. He wore his navy suit, a white shirt, a red tie. His scuffed deck shoes were polished to a dull shine. The coroner's report said he'd been dead about sixteen hours. Cause of death — carbon monoxide poisoning.

Dolores came right away on the train, called my parents and made all the other calls. The funeral is hard to remember. My mother wanted an open casket and the funeral director said that would be possible. Possible. Dolores shines in the face of crisis, but then she was a nurse in intensive care before our second child was born. Finally she quit because of all the shift work. Anyway, she brought me some sleeping-pills and taught me a grounding exercise she learned in her yoga class at the YWCA.

"Sit here and put your feet on the floor," she said. "Now, rest your hands on your knees. Feel yourself in the chair, Brian. Feel your spine and your legs, the back of your legs.

Be aware of your feet touching the floor and your hands on your legs. Now breathe in through your nose. Exhale slowly through your mouth. Say to yourself I am here. I am okay."

I did the exercise with her a few times in the coffee room, upstairs at the funeral home. My mother stayed with the casket the whole time and Dad stood sentinel at the front door. Dolores gave me a cigarette after a while, and we sat on the green leather couch, drinking hot coffee and smoking, listening to the hum of the small fridge in the corner.

We stayed at a hotel downtown. Dolores had a long bath, then slept in the king-sized bed while I paced, smoking and staring through the sheers at the fog-shrouded lights of the city.

Dolores suggested we go to the registrar's office at the university, make sure no paperwork would be sent to the house. I had a hard time talking that week, not that I was on the verge of breaking down, just that I couldn't get anything to come out. Every time someone talked to me I nodded a lot, which made them cry and pat my arm, probably thinking I was feeling exactly what they were saying. No, not that — in fact, I hardly heard what anyone was saying. So Dolores went into the office and left me to wander around campus. No one took any notice of me shuffling up and down the pathways between the buildings, stopping to peer at cornerstone inscriptions. Students walked in groups of two and three, wore shorts to hurry spring, and girls carried armloads of books against their chests. I had attended this same university all those years ago — hard to imagine, much less believe, given the weight of the day. And then Dolores was at my side, telling me Evan had withdrawn from all his classes two weeks earlier.

When we got to the house my mother was out, Dad in the basement. Dolores checked the closet while I scoured the desk and bookcase. Neat, tidy, all but bare of his mark. No letters or notes. His clothes bothered me the most. Sweatshirts and sneakers, everything orderly. In truth I wanted to take all of Evan's clothes with me, push them in suitcases and throw them in the trunk of the car, take them home. I didn't say anything, though, as Dolores pushed the closet door gently shut; I didn't say a thing.

Two months after the funeral, Dolores called me at work and told me to come home. She passed me the letter. Evan's neat handwriting.

> Dear Brian,
> I'm sorry for everything. All I hope is that
> you will understand.
> With love, Evan.

That was all. It was dated a week before I had found the body and the postmark showed it had been mailed from Brighton, in England. Dolores called Mom and asked if she could find and mail us Evan's old address book. She didn't explain why, Mom didn't ask and to my knowledge that was the last time my mother spoke directly of Evan. Dolores wrote to a name and address in Brighton and a young girl called us a week later. She'd been here on an exchange trip and had met Evan when he was in grade twelve. She had no inkling of the suicide. They had only exchanged two letters, nothing of any consequence. In the last letter he had enclosed the letter for me, asking her to mail it for him. Evan had told her I'd be pleased at the English stamps and post-mark.

Spring seems so thwarted here, a day of sunshine and melt-
ing, then back to cold weather, gloves and hats. I've been
considering requesting a transfer to another school, possibly even a high school. Went to the gym at lunch today to
watch the girls' basketball team practise. Our phys-ed
teacher is a bit of a bastard, typical coach, yelling at the kids,
his face red and angry. It would have been nice to close my
eyes — only the sounds of sneakers on the gym floor, sudden squeaking with the turns and jumps, the scent of
adolescent sweat and effort, sometimes a waft of perfume.
As I couldn't very well close my eyes, I simply leaned back
in the bleachers with a book, stared at the words long
enough to lose focus and blur the page into grey dots. Can't
seem to eat lunch these days.

Most times I think I'll never understand Evan's death, but
days like this I feel some inkling of the grief, maybe the grief
of solitude. Must not have been easy for him growing up
alone in a house with two old people. He was five when I
left home. I think Evan knew then what I am only beginning
to glimpse now, a kind of obscene futility that mocks our
wasting time, wasting air. Last year I was admitted to the
emergency department twice, chest pain, thought I was having a heart attack, thought I was dying. Dolores asked me
not to go, told me it was likely pulled muscles in the chest
wall or stress, so I ended up driving there myself. Felt so stupid watching the intern connect me to the EKG machine,
the tape spill out the side with proof of the even, steady
rhythm of my heart. To save face we all agreed on the diag-
nosis of heartburn, something I ate. It's not that I want to
die, I don't. The subdued politeness of middle-age suffocates
me though — the implicit expectation I will do the right
thing, mow the lawn, get the car oil changed, mend the
screen door, say the right thing. It's almost as if I'm carrying

around my body but inside me everything is changing; if I could talk to Evan now I feel I would have some measure of relief. To put one foot in front of the other, teach my classes, get through the days at school, is all I can manage, just barely it seems.

The girl in my class, Lisa, gave me a present last week. I was on yard duty and she came and stood beside me on the concrete steps of the school. She has green eyes with flecks of gold near the centre and she looked at me quizzically, as if she sensed my sadness, and I told her some of the story of Evan. The next day she gave me a small parcel wrapped in green tissue, a seashell and another poem. Then the bell rang and the classrooms started to fill. She sits in the row nearest the windows, second seat from the front.

> *What about this box of pictures,*
> *Lies, black and white lies*
> *Only one worth saving —*
> *Christmas tree on a table*
> *Four years old, sitting underneath*
> *Plaid pants and a striped shirt*
> *Little white undershirt showing too*
> *Holding a puppet, a clown*
> *Clowns, lies, black and white*
> *Laughing, crying, scary*
> *This is the only smiling picture*
> *Not just a trick, fake picture*
> *No, this one is real*
> *Holding the puppet, other hand on chest,*

Smiling, real and true and it hurts to look —
Silver icicles on my head like angel's fingers.

Tomorrow Dolores will phone the memorial in to the newspaper, all those miles away. My mother will no doubt clip it out and paste it into the spiral-bound notebook she keeps beside her cookbook.

COMFORT FOOD

The chestnuts form a mountain of odd-shaped brown nuggets, between the Christmas tangerines and plastic lemons. Without the price sign I wouldn't know what they are. Weird that the local grocery store bothers bringing them in — even nuts in the shell are rare in my neighbourhood. Holiday food is usually chips and dip, jars of sweet mixed pickles and salty peanuts in a tin. Being as it's Christmas Eve, the price of the chestnuts is slashed way down, and for no good reason I half-fill a five-pound bag and take it to the cash register.

At my house we eat tinned fruit, usually fruit cocktail — pale bloated grapes and cherries with leathery skin, all swimming in a pool of syrup. Fried bologna, corned beef and cabbage, chicken haddie, hamburger, boiled potatoes, greyish-green tinned peas. A lot of people my age, sixteen, are very fussy and on diets. I never gain any weight so I eat pretty much what I want. The high school has a cafeteria — most days I get milk and jello and eat my sandwich but on

Fridays I buy whatever is the special of the day. People are a lot more snobby than they were in junior high; that's because there are more *money people* at the school — because it has high academic standards. If you sit at someone's table to eat and they don't know you, they never make any conversation. I always take a book. When I'm sitting home on our chrome suite, scuffing my feet on the linoleum, my concern isn't the menu but whether my mother will notice if I miss my midnight curfew on the twenty-fifth, Christmas night.

Christmas is never very good. Mostly just more fighting, more drinking than usual. However, this particular Christmas Eve the house is kind of quiet. Two days ago my father threw the decorated tree out the front door. It stayed on the lawn for everyone to see until he went up to bed. We could hear him snoring like he does when he's drunk. Then my mother and I brought the tree back in the house and fixed it up, threw out the broken ornaments but there weren't a lot — we mainly use those satin balls, which, believe it or not, are plastic on the inside.

In the row-housing where we live, the best place to be is at the end, because then you only have neighbours making noise on one side. There are three bedrooms and I have my own room, the middle sized bedroom. My two brothers used to share it but they're both moved out now. (Gordie is in Alberta and Dan lives uptown in a rooming-house.) The tiny bedroom has the ironing-board set up in it, a single bed, boxes of dishes, all kinds of junk. My father has the master bedroom and my mother sleeps on the fold-out couch in the living-room, when she sleeps at all. Mostly she drinks cup after cup of tea at the kitchen table, and smokes until the ashtray gets full, then empties it into an old tin beside the kitchen sink. She knows I smoke now too and she doesn't care.

The fact that the holiday blow up has already happened is a relief. After a big scene usually come three or four days of silence, no one saying much of anything to anyone else — the pattern never changes. I kind of enjoy these times when I can move through the house less carefully. No matter how you look at it, this Christmas the timing is good. Most years the blow up isn't until Christmas Eve — then I end up hiding out in my bedroom, eating barbecue chips, reading and trying to make the words drown out the yelling downstairs. Yes, this holiday has more of the makings of the kind I've always wanted — like the songs.

I decide to keep the chestnuts a secret, which is pretty easy. Mom's gone to her sister's place and won't be home until after midnight church service. My father has gone to bed early, likely not to reappear until morning to sit, gloomy, watching us unwrap presents. Not that he doesn't get presents of his own, because he does. Christmas is pretty much the worst day of the year for him — a combination of lousy memories and a severe hangover, no doubt. Plus he probably realizes we fall so far short of your ideal Christmas family. It's not as if you can push the rest of the year aside and pretend for one day. Hardly. My mother tries but her heart's not in it any more. If I had my way, I'd rather spend Christmas with my brother Dan in the rooming-house.

Our kitchen radio doesn't work great. There's a whole lot of static turning the thing on and then it seems to have only two options, really quiet or really loud. I finally get it working and adjusted to quiet, mainly Christmas music — what else would you expect? The decorations uptown are cool but too bad there's no snow. There are huge wreaths all around the bandstand and the store windows are something else. I could spend ages uptown just looking at stuff. Sometimes the songs make me think they're about this place. That one, "Silver Bells", when they sing about the decorations *dressed in holiday style*, I honest to God think they're singing about this exact city. That probably sounds stupid but it makes me feel in the mood, Christmassy, kind of excited in spite of everything. Looking out the window I can see the night is cold and clear, not a cloud in sight. Spreading the chestnuts on a baking pan, I wait for the oven to preheat. After sliding the tray in, I pour a glass of pop and sit back to read *Reader's Digest*.

Halfway through an article about a boy trapped underneath a flipped canoe I hear a noise, a kind of miniature explosion, then another explosion, quickly followed by two muffled thuds. Turning on the oven light, I peer through the grease-covered glass. The chestnuts are exploding, just like popcorn. As I watch, a shiny hull splits and the mealy white centre goes flying right onto the oven element.

Opening the oven door, I grab a tea-towel and flap it around, trying to clear the smoke as another chestnut explodes, shooting out the door and hitting the side of the fridge. I slam the door shut and turn off the heat. Then I prop open the window with a pot to let the smoke clear. My father only sleeps well when he's drunk, so I turn off the radio and listen, listen, but his snoring stays the same.

It takes almost an hour to clean up the mess and I burn my arm on the oven door. The worst part is scraping the burnt bits off the element with a kitchen knife, the noise vibrating in my fillings. I put everything in the garbage except for the chestnuts that didn't explode. These I put in an empty jar and stash it in my knapsack. By the time my mother comes home from church there is no sign of anything, and I'm asleep.

My boyfriend, Matthew, picks me up at six-thirty the next night. He's twenty-one, a cabinet-maker with asthma. The sawdust almost kills him and the week before Christmas has been really busy. Blanket boxes are all the rage and Matthew's been sanding up a storm. Once I stopped in to see him after school and he was coughing so hard that all the veins in his neck stood out. I think the asthma keeps him skinny. Not that he isn't good-looking, because he is, light hair and dark brown eyes. In fact, he looks a lot like that ballet dancer, Baryshnikov, but not the same legs, of course.

I love the story of how I met Matthew. First I should say I was not technically a virgin when we met. The year before, when I was in grade nine, I'd gone to this party. Not the kind of thing I usually do, but once someone asked me I figured I'd go and see what I was missing. The whole thing was stupid, everyone wrecked or at least pretending to be wrecked on one or two puffs off a joint. Someone was throwing up in the bathroom, missing the toilet completely. I know because I opened the door. Music was cranked and people were necking, heading off to bedrooms and locking the doors. I was looking at a potted tree when someone spoke to me, his name is Jonathan and he was in my home room.

"Like the tree?" he asked.

I shrugged and took a drink from the bottle of beer he offered me.

"Val's mother planted it from a grapefruit seed on her honeymoon."

He knew more about the house and people than I did because he lived on the same street. People owned their houses here instead of renting, and it was a way nicer area than the courts where I live. Inviting people from the courts was sort of risky business, the danger being one of us might break a window, wreck some furniture, start a fight; people from the courts were supposed to be tough and not know how to handle nice objects. We got invited for the same reason the rich kids stole their parents' liquor or set up the 8mm projector and watched porn movies they found in their parent's closets — the thrill of danger, the forbidden.

To make a long story short, Jonathan and I ended up in a loft over the garage, necking, and then we did it. No big deal. Better to get it over with, I figured. The worst part was afterwards, trying to find my underwear and pulling it on, the awful wetness between my legs soaking through onto my jeans. Jonathan just lay there on his stomach, his head on his crossed arms, looking at an old dartboard.

"I wish Chris could see me now," he said.

Can you believe it? Chris was the captain of the boys' basketball team, he was in our class too. Unreal. I didn't say anything, just climbed down the ladder and walked home alone, had to wait until morning to have a bath. Soaking in the tub, I decided then and there not to go out with anyone I went to school with. Ever.

The next day my brother Dan called and invited me to go hear him at a coffee-house uptown. He plays guitar, not very well, but he plays. I took the bus and got off not far from his place. The street he lives on has a furrier's, gold letters on the window, mannequins with big fur hats. An old woman was coming out of the rooming-house as I climbed the steps. She held the door for me, and you'd better believe it's a heavy door. The hallway has faded wallpaper, red roses and vines. If I were younger I'd want to slide down the banister because it's so long, and very dark wood, almost black, with fussy spindle things, like my Aunt Georgina's pineapple-post bed. Dan opened the door before I knocked, must have heard me in the hall. I would have liked to stay in his room for a bit, everything is so compact there. He has a two-burner hotplate and a little sink, and the bathroom is down the hall. The one window faces the roof of the next building, and he says all he can smell in the summertime is hot tar but he doesn't mind it, the smell is something he's used to now and he actually kind of likes it. Well, Dan was in a big hurry to get to the coffee-house, and nudged me to-wards the stairs with his guitar case.

The coffee-house was behind the library, a fifteen-minute walk. You wouldn't know the place was there if someone hadn't told you. I don't know what it used to be, but inside was one giant room with tables and church pews for seats. They got them from an old church being torn down. It seemed weird to watch pews full of people smoking and drinking coffee, but that's how it was. We ordered hot choco-late from the little counter near the door — there were no waitresses — and took the drinks to a table near the front. The first guy played some song about a hole in Daddy's arm where all the money went, something like that. Then it was Dan's turn. He played "Rocky Raccoon", and he does a pretty good job on that one. While he was playing I noticed this guy smiling at me, sitting with a couple. It was Matthew, but I didn't know it then. God, he looked great, and he kept star-ing at me, so I'd look away, watch Dan or stir my hot chocolate, then I'd look back and there he'd be still looking at me. Imagine how I freaked out when he called me the next night. He'd asked Dan for my phone number, knew him because Dan sometimes drove a truck delivering furniture for the place Matthew worked.

We went to a movie the first time we went out. He's very quiet and I like that. Plus he's not all groping like people my age. When he kisses me it's like the movies only better, not like being attacked. Just slow and nice. He stops sometimes and just touches my face, like he's lost and trying to find his way home. We used to drive to a beach on the outskirts of town, sometimes build a fire in the sand. One time he brought me a wooden box he'd made from bird's-eye maple; the top was kind of a swirly design. Shortly after that we did it, not all cramped in the car but in the woods, and when I am old I will count that as the first real time. The moon was half full and even though it was getting cold, late October, mostly I'll remember how safe I felt, how happy.

We drive to a motel, one in a string of places for tourists who don't know enough to turn around and get out of town. Matthew goes to the office and rents the room while I wait in the car, blowing into my hands — his heater is broken.

Fifteen minutes later we're naked, sitting on the bumpy mattress, the blue chenille spread pulled up to our waists. Matthew has cranked the heat; the fan is blowing hot dusty air into the room. *Miracle on 34th Street* is on the television and I watch it while he rolls a joint from the bag of grass he brought. He doesn't drink, claims he doesn't enjoy the feeling. Fine by me. He likes dope, even though the smoke bothers his asthma. Whenever a bad bout of wheezing comes on, he gets the blue puffer from the pocket of his flannel shirt, shakes it, inhales and holds his breath. I count out loud but he hardly ever gets past eight because he can't breathe deeply by then.

Half-watching the movie, we smoke the joint and I grab our knapsacks, pull them onto the bed. He has brought chips, ginger ale and a bag of peppermints. I add to the pile two candy canes from our tree. The colours have run; the plastic wrappers are sticky from the tree being out on the lawn.

Then I pull out the jar of chestnuts. They look like rocks and when I take the lid off the smell of burnt wood fills the room.

When I tell him how I tried to roast them Matthew laughs, a quiet, gentle laugh, one of the reasons I love him. We bite into a few, the blackened skins giving way to cold, oily centres, then get up and spit them into the garbage can beside the television stand. The peppermints take away the burnt taste.

Matthew tells me I have the best body in the free world, then he always says, "Whip me, beat me, make me write bad cheques." It's a joke, we don't actually do weird things. Just his sense of humour. Sometimes he talks about his work, router bits and finishes, and I don't mind listening. In fact, it's kind of interesting. He's very good at woodworking because he has a lot of patience. Plus he is never in a rush, never.

He drops me off at my place just after midnight, only a few minutes past my curfew. My mother's at the table playing solitaire and I sit down across from her. She doesn't say anything, just pushes her cigarette pack towards me. I take one and strike a match, inhale, smoke mingling with the smell of sex on my fingers.

THE COPULATORY GAZE

Pigeons formed a grey queue along the bandstand roof, bodies pressed together for warmth. Lunch-hour traffic circled the city square, cars starting and stopping, and above everything hung the sickly-sweet smell of bus exhaust mixed with the odour of the mill. After Lisa finished her sandwich she tossed the crusts onto the walkway and the pigeons came, a living cloud moving to the ground, shoving and pecking to get at the bits of bread.

Learning about the Great Fire in high school had transformed Lisa's perceptions of the square. She could no longer sit alone without picturing frenzied crowds, women with crying babies held close, men carrying trunks and pieces of furniture, the noise, the smoke, the terror, everyone watching what must have seemed the whole world roar and crash, Armageddon. She went to the library several times, the museum too, searching for more details, studying the grainy photos for glimpses of human grief, but all she found were pictures of rubble, stubborn stone left standing in a sea of charred and splintered timbers. Some days she felt what seemed to be the sorrow of the entire city, a place that daily grew more unbearable.

From her waitressing job, she banked all she was able, emptying the brown pay envelope onto the teller's counter, the change that was her tips spilling and rolling. She enrolled in several courses at the business college, typing, accounting, shorthand. The typing teacher was a furious woman, her anger seeming to fuel her own typing speed, at which the students marvelled.

"This can be yours," the woman would say of her skill, pausing to push a stray hair into her tight bun or straighten a bobby pin.

She stood at the front of the class, a yardstick in hand, and beat the rhythm, made the students chant the letters like prayers, *A, S, D, F, J, K, L, semicolon*. Lisa did very well in typing, so well, in fact, the teacher occasionally offered her a pinched smile — more a grimace, really, but nevertheless slight encouragement for her efforts. Everything was a rush at that time; washing pantyhose in the sink at home, racing to catch the bus, to classes, to her job. Lisa had one goal, that being to leave town before she was too late. Too late for what? Too late to leave, too mired in the place, unable to even dream of anywhere else.

Some of the patrons at the restaurant were Lisa's classmates from high school, most of them attending the local university. They came to eat in groups, sometimes couples, and waved to her, embarrassed to have her serve them; they tipped her too much. The dark interior, the tablecloths, heavy navy curtains, gave the place a certain ambience; businessmen, women whose husbands didn't care what they spent on lunch, these were the usual patrons. The diner

down the street, greasy windows, booths full of loud teen-
agers, plates of fries and gravy appearing again and again,
was the sort of place where tips were meagre, not from
meanness but simply out of need. So Lisa didn't mind seeing the people she'd graduated with, didn't acknowledge
their embarrassment, but stood straight and ready to take
each order or offer suggestions from the menu.

"Are you coming to university next year?" they'd ask her
and she would shrug, answer, "Probably."

The first night Stan came to the restaurant, Lisa was finishing her shift, trying not to think of her feet, the ache in the
small of her back. He sat at a table near the rear, close to the
lounge, put his briefcase and coat on an empty chair. She
knew he was watching her, could feel his gaze as she cleared
dishes, wiped the tables clean. These men came and went,
married men who flirted with the waitresses, made stupid
jokes, stretched their egos through exchanged glances. On
occasion Lisa would follow the lead, nod and smile, wait for
the inevitable next visit and the next, until finally an offer
was made, dinner out, somewhere nice.

It came as no surprise after the first time that dinner was
followed by some furtive groping in a car, tearing and pulling at clothes, moaning, and afterwards, only after
everything, apologies served up by the man.

"Jesus, sorry about that. Don't know what got into me. I'm
not usually like this. I have a wife and family. Couldn't help
myself. You should be more careful. Oh God, oh God, oh
God."

And during all of it Lisa would feel herself watching everything from a great distance, the hungry flesh, the pale torsos
moving beneath the dim light of the moon or sometimes a
streetlight. She wondered if they thought she was amazed,
stupid even, taken unaware by the inevitable course of

events. She purposely made it easy for them, helped them along every practised step of the way.

"I'm leaving here next year," she would tell them.

"Leaving? Jesus, don't say that."

But of course that was the safety net; no fear of hysterical phone calls in the middle of the night, of clinging or, God forbid, a young husband showing up with a hunting rifle or a baseball bat.

"Yes, I'm going out west to work. To B.C."

"Their gain," one man mumbled, fumbling to get his zipper up.

For a year after Matthew moved to Montreal, Lisa dated no one. He wrote for a few months, told her not to write back as his address would be changing. He'd gone with two friends, hitch-hiking, seeing the world. Didn't seem they got any farther than Montreal, judging from the postmarks, but then the letters stopped altogether. Lisa threw them out, pushed them into the garbage in the kitchen, beneath oily sardine tins and carrot scrapings.

She started working nights at the restaurant during her last year at high school, helping in the kitchen. If not for the money she'd have been happy to stay in the kitchen, scraping plates, loading and emptying the dishwasher, eating cheese omelettes made by Eddie, the cook, who sometimes picked his ears with a wooden matchstick. Eddie urged her to get out front where the money was, the tips.

"Nothing good come back here," he told her, "'cept a hunk of bone or fat some poor bastard couldn't swallow. Buy good shoes and get out there."

So she did. After graduation she moved to the front, put on the navy jumper, white blouse and apron that constituted the waitress uniform. Much of what she already knew in life proved useful: move quickly and quietly, never lose your balance, smile just a little no matter how you feel, the customer is always right.

Of all the customers, the ones that truly amazed her were the mothers coming for lunch with young daughters after a shopping trip. They would carry many parcels, boxes and bags from Scovill Brothers and Calps, and Lisa liked to imagine what was inside, perhaps party dresses with lace collars and stiff crinoline skirts, maybe a pair of patent-leather shoes wrapped in tissue and nestled in a box, maybe even hats with ribbons. Sometimes these women wore fur coats and were unwilling to have them hung on the coat-rack, preferred instead to loosen the dark leather buttons and keep the coats perched on their shoulders, looking for all the world like prey being attacked by a wild animal. The little girls were fussy, smoothing skirts and touching hair, mimicking their mothers, pursing their lips, folding their hands as they waited for the food to appear. Lisa knew what the future held for these girls, based on what she had seen happen at her high school. More clothes than you could imagine, different outfits all the time; real jewellery, gold rings with birthstones, opals, amethysts; good haircuts and thick velvet hairbands; dates with boys who played soccer, football, rugby. Boys the mothers would approve of, *yes ma'am, no ma'am, this is my father's car, sir*. These girls would marry at the appropriate time, not because they were pregnant, never. These girls would get diamond rings from Birks for Christmas; then would come wedding showers and china patterns and bridesmaids' dresses, pastel silk dresses with shoes dyed to match. Working at the restaurant, Lisa could watch these things unfold, serve tables of young women her own age as they made lists, laughing sometimes behind their hands, and smiling, always smiling.

Sometimes when her shift was over Eddie would tap on the small window of the swinging door to the kitchen, beckon to her.

"Want me to make you something? Come, sit, tell me about being young 'cause I forget." He'd tap his temple with his finger as he said it, grinning, showing gaps of missing teeth. She would grin back and agree to look at the picture of his new grandchild, a wrinkled fat red face, thick black hair standing straight up, agree that the child was beautiful, beautiful. But more often than not she would hurry off, rush to typing class or home to prepare for the next day.

Stan came to the restaurant frequently after his first appearance, at times spreading work papers on the table, frowning as he flipped pages, absent-mindedly eating his meal, ordering a second drink or perhaps a third. He never spoke to her except to place his order, ask for an ashtray. One day after he left, as she cleaned his table, she noticed the drink coaster, a ten-dollar bill folded in half beneath it. Written on the coaster — *Do you know how lovely you are*?

Carefully she folded the money again and shoved it into the pocket of her uniform, with the coaster. Later that night — much later, when her parents were both asleep — she turned on her bedroom light and looked at the coaster, traced her fingers over the indentations made by the pen. Lovely, lovely, what was lovely? What was love? She'd finally tried to tell Matthew she loved him, just before he left, and his face had been pained. As soon as she said it, crying, she wanted to pull the words back inside, could not bear to look at him. Sometimes the men she went with spoke of love in guttural murmurings, as if obligated to bring the word, some implied decency, into the frantic coupling. But lovely was different, better, safer. She brought her hands to cover her face, felt her eyelashes flutter against her palms — lovely, could she be, lovely?

Appearances always matter, Stan told younger men working for him. He was a stern mentor, a bully at times, but the young men learned more from his teachings than they would have liked to admit. Most important, they learned timing, learned about waiting, not rushing, allowing the client to feel the decision was his own creation, not one force fed.

Stan gave his teenaged daughter the same advice, chose his wife's clothes. On weekdays he wore dark wool trousers, tweed jackets, plain shirts which he purchased twice a year on trips to Boston. At times he affected a jocular air, should the situation support one — a weak English accent, a feigned boyishness that he believed was especially appealing to women. His affairs, he reasoned, were validation of the appeal — it seemed to him that certain women, not so much beautiful as handsome, seemed to end up subtly pursuing him after the initial baiting. He chose women with several concerns in mind, not wanting to risk his marriage, not wanting any fuss. He favoured slender legs, narrow hips; was a stickler for hygiene, secretly disgusted by men or women with unkempt nails. The two things that drew him to Lisa were her slender hands and the way she glanced down as he ordered his meal, a trace of smile, pleased, he guessed.

The next day Lisa went to the City Market to buy a bag of dulse from the fish stand. Just inside the large wrought-iron gates an old woman stood selling daffodils wrapped in newspaper. A young man played a guitar, no recognizable tune, only chords repeated over and over. The open case at his feet had a smattering of coins dotting the red lining, and Lisa leaned down to add some change from her pocket, then stood and moved past the entrance to the centre aisle of the market. Sloping from top to bottom, the market ran a whole city block, three long aisles full of vendors, vegetables, knitted and crocheted goods, farm-fresh eggs, tie-dyed scarves, postcards. The permanent stalls were built against the walls and at the head and foot of the market. Here you could be offered a slice of cheddar, sharp and clean, on the edge of a huge gleaming knife, or have a haddock held forth in display, the sightless black eyes shining with slivers of ice.

Lisa stopped at a fish stall to watch lobsters crawling over one another in the dark water. Just as she was about to open her purse to pay for the small brown bag of dulse, she felt a hand at her elbow.

"May I?"

Turning, she saw him, didn't know his name, was not certain of the question. In her mind she heard the singsong children's game — *Mother may I take three giant steps, Mother may I take one baby step, Mother may I, Mother may I, you didn't say Mother may I.*

Stan pushed a bill across the painted counter before Lisa could answer and steered her away from the stall, towards the doors, outside. They moved to the traffic lights, crossed into the square, walked to an empty bench and sat down, Lisa holding her purse and the dulse tightly on her lap, like the bag ladies who sat in the square cursing and spitting at no one, hugging meagre possessions, stamping their feet territorially.

The conversation was banal on the surface, one-sided, Stan gesturing, smiling, and Lisa only nodding, uncertain what was expected. Most of her consorts appeared at night, usu-

ally after finishing dinner with their families at home, pushing away from the table, excusing themselves to attend to
overdue office work, late night, late. They came to the restaurant, sat in the lounge drinking and smoking until Lisa's
shift ended, and then waited for her to balance her cash and
fetch her coat. She saw these men at night, and if she did
see them, later, in the daytime, accidentally on the street,
they would cough and look away or duck into the nearest
store. Once the line had been crossed they rarely returned
to the restaurant. Security arose from their predictability;
each would move according to rules of inaction. Sitting in
the square, Lisa felt exposed, felt that somehow this infor-
mal meeting held more danger than all her previous
encounters. She became nervous, looking side to side, chewing her bottom lip.

"I'd like to see more of you."

What did that mean? More of her now, later, just plain more
of her, more often?

When she didn't answer, Stan assumed agreement on her
part and pointed to the hotel directly in front of them, facing the square and across the street from the restaurant. A
crew of workers had arrived from Maine to sandblast the
limestone exterior of the hotel, to lift decades of grime, li-
chen, shadows of ivy branches long since removed. Large
sheets of canvas draped several windows, covered the awn-
ing, and because it was lunch-hour men sat on the planks of
the scaffolding, feet over the edge, drinking from thermoses.
Stan told her he would be staying at the hotel on Friday
night, alone, and perhaps she might like to stop in and pay
a visit.

A month later Lisa bought a pair of shoes, chocolate-brown leather as smooth as the nape of a baby's neck, high heels. Her hand shook a little as she counted out the money to pay for the shoes, more than she had ever spent on any single item in her life. And why? Because Stan hated flat shoes, told her how an arched foot tensed the leg muscle, provided a more pleasing line.

While she folded her clothes — a skirt, cream-coloured blouse — he sat in a chair near the hotel window, drinking sherry from a pewter flask, rubbing his hand over the engraved initials. Sometimes he asked her to stop, to hold a position, and she did, muscles cramping, while he watched.

Most of the time she tried to remember to breathe, a thing that now required effort on her part — to breathe, aware of the weight of his body, which so often seemed to empty her of breath. She usually had a quick bath afterwards while he ran a sinkful of warm water, soaped his hands, placed a towel on the edge of the sink as protection against the cold enamel. He glanced over his shoulder, met her eyes in the mirror as she moved the white facecloth over her legs, shivering slightly. His movements were caressing, soaping his genitals, cupping handfuls of water to rinse himself until the suds ran pale and cloudy.

"That's the thing about women," he said to her face in the mirror and she stopped washing to listen. "See, it's easy for men. Women can never get really clean, no matter how hard they try."

GOOD COURAGE

Reg made several trips to the car in the narrow alley between the tenement buildings. He packed his tools in the
car trunk, emptied nails from his pockets, sorting them by
size into the blue cardboard boxes nestled within a wooden
crate. The smell of the fire-job clung to his clothes, his hands,
his hair. The fire had been small, mostly smoke damage. He'd
spent the day nailing strapping to the ceiling in preparation
for ceiling tiles. No doubt the next tenant would always
sense the odour of the fire — the same scent as when a wet
wind blows down a chimney, over a bed of blackened em-
bers.

Before heading for the tavern he stopped at his sister's
home. From the back seat of the car he retrieved a grocery
bag; bananas, oranges, apples, pears, and a small box of
Ganong chocolates. It was not unusual for him to take items
to Georgina; perhaps twice a month he appeared. "Things
that were on sale," he always told her, though this was not

true. He made his purchases not at the regular grocery store, but at Joe's Fruit Basket; a store specializing in gifts sent to hospitals. She likes nice things, he reasoned, as he carefully sorted through piles of fruit to find pieces with no bruises.

"How is my boy?" Georgina asked as he placed the bag inside the front door of her house.

"Good, but I can't stay," he answered.

Georgina knew he was going to the tavern, she knew all of this and more, and she placed most of the blame on Agnes. He could have had his pick of the lot, she thought, pick of the lot.

"You go ahead, dear," she told him. "I expect you need a break, working like you do. We all work like that, this whole family though, don't we? In the blood. Never mind, go along. Thank you for being good to your sister. Bye."

And he walked back to his car, ducking his head into his collar.

For thirty years the tavern interior never changed, until the laws regarding women in drinking establishments were altered. Then came a small stick-on sign purchased from the dime store — "Ladies". There was little discussion as to where the women's bathroom would go, the only option being a closet near the fire escape. The cook had argued in favour of the storage locker near the kitchen, no doubt hoping to look up from chopping onions and watch a parade of young women pass by, but the board of health wouldn't allow rest-rooms so near the kitchen.

It took Reg the better part of two days to rough up the job, get studs in place for some new gyprock and a dropped ceiling. His friend came and did the plumbing; turned out to be easier than anyone expected. When the white enamel paint on the door dried, Reg peeled the paper backing from the metal sign and pushed it onto the wood, aiming for centre but going slightly askew.

No one used the bathroom for weeks, almost two months. Elsewhere in the city's taverns, women were using bathrooms, taking advantage of the change in liquor laws that allowed them unescorted into real drinking establishments. Most of them were young, just past the legal drinking age, and they went out in groups of three and four, in bright minidresses, cork-soled platform shoes and plastic jewellery. Depending on the tavern, they were greeted with sarcasm, enthusiasm or not at all, simply ignored.

Reg's tavern had a reputation for serious drinking; it was a place where you could sit in good company with men who measured a day's success by sweat. Most of the regulars came daily after work, and left before the night crowd came — a younger group, more prone to fights, especially on the weekends. No, for the most part the regulars didn't come on the weekends or stay late into the night. They came after work, settled into the same table with the same group of men, bought draft in a perpetual rotating pattern. Reg had few friends, but some enemies. The friends would be quick to jump to his defence, speak of him as *a hard worker. Pays his way, likes his beer, full of stories.* Enemies would recall a loud man, quick to anger. They would say he was a mean drunk who only laughed at his own jokes and had no patience.

Each morning he rose at dawn, dressed and shaved. Left the house after breakfast, which he prepared himself. Just before he left his wife got up, had a cigarette sitting on the side of the bed, came downstairs and poured what was left in the teapot into a cup as he picked up his lunchbox and left.

For years Reg had worked under a prosperous contractor who had nothing but praise for his carpentry. Never missed a day for sickness, always the first one on the job. The contractor had once hoped that Reg would teach some of the younger carpenters the detail work, but this arrangement ended the day he threw a mitre-box at a young man, barely missing his head and gouging a freshly built window frame. After that he was allowed to work alone, undisturbed. A fight over wages ended the relationship and Reg left to work alone, odd-jobbing with people who knew his work from past experience. Most of the time there was enough work, though winters were slow.

Working for himself, he chose to start early, lay down the tools at three-thirty and head for the tavern. His friend John was there every day waiting for him, nursing a beer and looking at the newspaper. John hadn't worked since he lost four fingers in the bandsaw but his wife was a nurse, they had one child. He shunned any outside advances of friendship, would not think of inviting other men to the table while he waited for Reg. When Reg appeared, John waved to the waiter, and four beer arrived while Reg used the bathroom, ran wet hands through his thick black hair. He came to the table and each afternoon unfolded predictably, the two men buying alternate rounds until John's wife came to pick him up after her shift at the hospital.

"That young fella was in here with that girl earlier," John says.

Reg takes a long swallow of beer, wipes foam from his lip with the back of his hand.

"Dress barely covering her, sitting there with her bare legs all stretched out," John continues.

"Did ya send her a beer?" Reg asks, scratching his neck.

"Now where would I get that kind of money? Like as not us end up getting in a fight, the fella come here picking a fight with me."

"Stupid son of a whore to bring her here. Would you bring Gloria here?" Reg asks.

"Lord Jesus no. I'm wanting to get as far away from her as I can. Jesus, that's for them young ones, think they gotta be takin' them everywhere they go."

"You musta got a good look."

John pushes back in his chair and drinks his beer in little sips, chuckling as he raises and lowers the glass. The door to the tavern opens and two women come in, both in tight jeans and tank tops, sunglasses. They sit at a table near the kitchen, where the light is brighter, smoke from liver, bacon and onions drifting over the kitchen's half wall in a wave.

"Look at that, look at them. Pros I reckon," John says.

"Buy 'em a drink," Reg goads him.

"Like as not they'd wanta come sit with us, get us all fired up, then Gloria'd come and maybe see them or something."

"I had so many women on the go at one time, had to play them all off each other. When Georgina worked at the drugstore, just after the war, had her get me six compacts, wrap 'em for Christmas presents."

John leans forward in his chair, cradles his beer glass in the circle of his arm, eyes shiny.

Reg continues. "Sure, I stopped at each girl's place on Christmas Eve to give the gifts, all of 'em wanting me to stay and sit with the parents, have a drink, and me saying I had to rush back to help at the house. Christ, all of them wet and groping me in the doorway, me trying to get my goddamned boots on and get the hell out so I could stop at the next place. Kept 'em all on the go for a year."

"The women always likes you, they sure like you."

"Look at them two there, fucking whores showing everything they got. Take that to bed and end up with the dose."

The two men sit back in their chairs and drink as the noise in the tavern grows, the door opening and more men arriving.

"Too bad yer boys never took up the trade, Reg," John says.

"Don't fucking start. Those boys never give me a minute's trouble. Look at that little bastard of yours, wrecking cars left and right, no Christly good."

"That's Gloria's doing, Reg, not mine. She's spoiled him, him the only one and all. Doesn't know how to say no, always giving him money behind my back — don't think I don't know, either."

"Eh, look there. Old Tony chatting the two of 'em up, look at that stupid bastard. They'll get some free drinks and he'll be mooching cab-fare home."

Reg signals the waiter who comes with four fresh beer.

"How're ya today, Reg?" he asks.

"Good, good. Listen, tell Darryl me and John want some food. I put the moulding up in the bastard's rec room and kitchen and the son of a whore still owes me for it. Tell him we want whatever he's doing for the night and tell him I'm not paying either." Reg has his money for the beer ready, passes it to the waiter. The tip is included, established years earlier.

Reg's sister, Georgina, has a row of blackberry bushes lining the small yard behind her house. At the back of her bedroom closet is a small crawlspace where she stores keepsakes — a christening dress, cards, some newspaper clippings and war letters from Reg. She was in her late thirties, engaged and still living at home, when he went overseas at age twenty-two. She would write to him every Friday night when she finished work at the drugstore, and twice a month she would pack a box with soap, chocolate and cigarettes to mail to him. She carried a photograph of him in her wallet. The letters from Reg, all on blue Armed Forces airmail paper, are taped in a notebook she bought at the drugstore, "Huge Scribbler, 5 cents". She has never reread them.

ঽ▪

August 24, 1944

Dear Georgina,

I just received two of your most welcomed letters also a gift box which was much appreciated as it was really a pleasure to wash with some good soap once more. The snaps of you were really good. Just to see someone with a smile after all the sights we have been through. I hope you don't get disappointed when you see my new rank which is a sapper. Nothing to worry about and I figure it's all for the best. Even as a sapper I'm getting along well with the men because when I was their sergeant I acted like a human being and have no regrets and am thankful for that. My officer is very good to me, he had a long talk with me yesterday and said he could use me to better advantage as an N.C.O. and wanted to know if I would except a hook once more with more to follow in the near future but I told him I was doing OK and would like to think it over and let him know later. You know its a hard job to be an N.C.O. in actual war as I found out. You have to tell men to do jobs and go places you wouldn't send your worst enemy in ordinary life, all the while there gone your worrying about them. In the meantime I'll be careful of those booby traps which are part of my business. Those pretty French girls you talk about are nearly all German agents. Boy I could tell you some wild stories about them but will wait until I get home. Thanks a million for your prayers. Please don't worry about me and tell Ma the same as I'm determined to come home safe and sound and lets hope soon. Remember me to all at home and thanks once more to the swellest sister in the world for all your kindness.

Your brother,
Reg

❧

September 1, 1944

Dear Georgina,

I guess its about time I was dropping you a few lines to let you know I'm still alive and kicking. I sure had some wild experiences lately but fortunately I'm none the worse for wear except for a little case of nerves which I guess will be alright with some rest while its quiet for a change. I received your letter of August 14th but we haven't seen any mail here in over a week. It seems we are moving fast and changing our camping area so often that our mail can't keep up with us and believe it or not were back on those famous compo rations again of hardtack and bully beef, but theres one consolation, we really have Jerry on the run now and after all that does help bring this damn thing to an end. I want to tell you how thankful I am for those lovely boxes you send as some of the contents really came in handy lately when I was hungry and had no way of getting food on account of heavy enemy fire. This letter leaves me fine and I hope it finds you the same so until later I'll say so long and chin up.

Your loving brother,
Reg

P.S. Give my regards to all at home.

༄

September 14, 1944

Dear Georgina,

I just received another of your most welcomed gift boxes, for which I wish to thank you very much. The dulse was a real surprise and it sure caused some fun around here. These fellows from the west never seen it before I guess from the way they talk. But I was explaining all the good points, like how it contained Iodine and was good for the gums, it was sure some fun. Thanks for those cookies as they sure come in handy especially when we are moving. I still have a hard time trying to convince the boys your my sister. You write so often and regular and send those lovely boxes so often that these fellows think your my wife or sweetheart. I hope I get one someday who is so faithful as you.

Love,
Reg

ða

September 20, 1944

Dear Georgina,

Sure glad to hear everything is O.K. with you all at home. I suppose you know by now we are really moving over here. I'll be like a gypsy by the time I get home. We just stay in one place long enough to clear some mines or build a bridge or fix some roads, then we move on to greener pastures or should I say more rubble. Were sure seeing a lot of France and it looks like we will soon have to learn a new language by the way things are going. We had a pretty tough job a little while ago when we made an assault crossing on the Seine River but once we got the infantry across they sure gave Jerry hell and it wasn't to long until all was peaceful again. I imagine that crossing will be about as close as we get to Paris as we seem to be heading in another direction. I have more than a hundred dollars in my pay book now as we have nowhere to spend it and I'll sure have a swell time when I do get my freedom. About those socks it would be O.K. to send one pair as thats all I can handle. We move so often we can't have too much to carry. This letter leaves me fine and hope it finds you and all at home the same so until later I'll say Au Revoir.

Love,
Reg

ε&

September 27, 1944

Dear Georgina,

I just received two of your letters today and was sure glad to hear everything is O.K. with all at home. Well your letters was the first news we had received in two weeks as we have been at the front and have sure seen some of the toughest action to be encountered in this war. More than likely you have now read about a Canadian Coy. of Engineers evacuating airborne troops from the west of Arnhem, well I can't explain it to you in detail but I will say I hope to God we never experience the likes of that again. We lost our officer and had quite a few casualties. You might know of a fellow Gerald Millard from Saint John, well he was lost to, most of them were drowned in the Rhine. But theres no doubt the English will think a hell of a lot of the Canucks after this. I wish you could have seen our boys the next morning, we were sure a sorrowful looking bunch. And I forgot to mention that Sgt. Williams got injured to. We lost everything we owned and didn't dare take time to look for it once it broke daylight. This Coy. has sure seen some drastic changes in personnel since we landed, but

fortunately for myself I have been lucky and had
nothing worse than a few cuts and scratches and
one time a bad case of nerves which I've pretty
well got over by now. And let me tell you we have a
religious fellow in our outfit who has hymn books
with him. We get together, Protestants and
Catholics and sing songs and he reads the bible and
then prays. And I haven't seen an Army chaplain
who can even come near him as far as sincerity
goes and I'm one boy who really believes in prayer.
I've seen it answered more than once. Well this
letter leaves me feeling fairly good and I hope it
finds you and all at home well. So until later I'll say
so long and good luck. Remember me to all at
home.

Love,
Reg

❧

December 25, 1944

Dear Georgina,

   Here it is Christmas day and the third one I've
spent away from home. But don't worry, I'm having
as good a time as can be expected considering
where I am. We just had a very nice dinner, yes
even turkey and all the trimmings. And after dinner
we were given a very good treat chocolate bars and
gum along with an orange and two bottles of beer.
So you see even though we are near the front we
didn't fare too bad. I'm sending you the menu of

our dinner along with some of my pals names for your scrapbook. The cartoon drawing of the shells coming through the wall will give you an idea of just what is going on up here but don't worry as we are pretty well used to it by now. I just came back off a very enjoyable leave in Brussels where I had some pictures taken so I'm sending you one. Heres hoping your all having a good time at home. So long for now and good luck.

Your brother,
Reg

❧

April 24, 1945

Dear Georgina,

Here I am back again in the old outfit, but as you will notice I am in number two platoon now. Guess who I just met as I'm writing this letter here on the street, none other than good old snuffy. Remember our major of the old 23rd (Major Slater). He just came over and shook hands with me, he's in charge of a field coy. here in town and we had quite a chat about the old 23rd. You should have seen the boys standing around with their mouths open as I had no hat on and was writing a letter so he was going by and called my name, well I just got up and shook hands with him like he was my best pal. No salute or nothing as I had no hat on. He sure treated me alright when he was with us and we formed a pretty close friendship. Some of the boys said you sure must know that major well, so I didn't let them know the difference. I said sure we went to school together (ha ha). Well I'm getting along O.K. and just now going to a fellow's house to see about buying some gold rings so I guess I'll sign off hoping this letter finds you and all at home well.

Your loving brother,
Reg

⁊

May 9, 1945

Holland
Victory
Dear Georgina,

Here it is at last, victory day, the day we have all been waiting for. And no doubt it has brought a great feeling of relief and happiness to us boys over here as well as many of their people at home. It is very hard to express my feelings right now that its all over but you can be sure they are feelings of great joy and thankfulness to God for having spared my life. Today I can join with you in thought and once again thank God for blessing me with such swell people at home as you have proven to be. I close now on this day of victory.

Your loving brother,
Reg

⁊

October 29, 1945

Dear Georgina,

   I just received your letter of September 28th and was sure glad to know all are well at home. You were saying your boss wanted to know which nationality had the best bed manners. Well to tell the truth that is hard to say. I can give him a rough idea of a few of them (hope I don't shock you both ha ha). To start with now the Limey or English are very coy although inclined to be a little rough as the evening wears on and the man wears out, and after a few nights with a man they begin to get very possessive, so naturally an old bachelor if he wants to remain such takes to his heels while he is still able. Now the Scotch and Irish after having known a man for a long time such as say three hours are inclined to be a little crude. They don't think nothing of parading around in the nude in front of a man which in time gets very monotonous and disgusting. I think they could stand a bit of teaching from the girls in Brussels on how to use their wiles so as to interest a man. Then comes the French well there are two types of them. One who keeps a fellow guessing as to just what her intentions are which gets a fellow a bit worried and wishing he were anywhere else but her buduior. Then there is the kid who after having been in bed awhile is liable to reach out for a chocolate bar (your optimal bait) and start munching just when you feel like getting some sleep. Then comes the Belgiques (boy are they something to write home about). You will find that her bed manners are as neat and trim as she is about herself and her clothes which is a sight to behold, especially in this war torn county need I say anymore (Woo Woo). And the Dutch who when possible are also very neat in appearance and dress but rather disappointing as far as bedside manners are concerned. When entering that holy sanctuary they lead you to believe you are headed for a wild session such as a boxer might expect when entering a ring. But after a short period you are liable to find them sound to sleep with that contented look even though your not. I guess that can be blamed on the war, after all they didn't get too much to eat and one does need plenty of calories to stand up to vigourous exercise (ha ha). I don't think I had better tell you anymore as you might get a bad opinion of your brother and wonder did I come over here to fight a war or study foreign women. I'll say this much that my choice would be a Brussels girl. I guess I've said enough for now, don't judge me too harshly because you know old soldiers are noted for their tall tales. Tell your boss once the novelty wears off you begin to realize they can't compare with our Canuck girls at home.

   Will say so long for now, remember me to all at home.

Your brother,
Reg

❧

December 22, 1945

Dear Georgina,

   I think this will be my last letter to you from over here and I can give you a pretty good idea when I'll arrive home. I just came back from a wild ten day leave to Manchester where I had a swell time. And when I came back there was your most welcomed Xmas parcel for which I want to thank you very much. We were told on parade this morning that we were confined to base until Dec. 27th when we will proceed to the boat. And we will be coming home either on the Cynthia or the Mauritania. It will take us about six days to cross the Atlantic so we should be in Halifax about Jan. 3rd. Yours truly should be home Jan. 4th or 5th. If possible I'll give you a ring from Halifax. Anyway, I think Ma will be getting a telegram telling of my arrival. All the boys here are so happy they don't seem to mind spending Xmas here. Really its hard to explain how we feel. Gosh were all just acting like a big bunch of kids. The main thing is we'll all be together again soon. So long for now and I'll be home very soon.

Love,
Reg

P.S. Please tell Ma to keep the Xmas tree up.

LAUNDRY

The clouds, pale grey and stagnant, are dense enough to trap the smell of the mill. Agnes glances out the kitchen window, sees Mrs. Murphy hanging a line of wash. There are new tenants across the court, arrived last week carrying boxes from the back of a rusted truck. Most of the neighbours moved to the courts close to twenty years ago, came from vermin-infested tenements sprawled across the city. Some managed to make a further move, to buy a small single dwelling, perhaps plant a hedge where the tiny lawn met the sidewalk. Others stayed, raised their families, drank any house down-payment or lost it at the racetrack, argued that anyone stupid enough to leave a place where you didn't have to mow the lawn was a fool.

The Fuller Brush man drives past the row of identical doors and parks, careful to keep his car away from the clothesline where Agnes's sheets trail, lank and still. Samples case banging his leg, he climbs the few steps and knocks on the door.

"Ed, come in," Agnes says.

She is pleased to see him, has purchased from him for more than a decade.

"Put that down," she says, pointing to his case. "I was just boiling the kettle for a fresh cup of tea."

Ed Rollings walks through a doorway to the dining-room. Despite a scratched dining-room set, the room is almost never used for meals. An ironing-board is permanently set up and a metal typing-table in the corner holds a basket of hair rollers, combs and elastics, and a can of hairspray. A large square mirror, salvaged from a bureau, is screwed into the wall above the typing-table. Ed places his case in front of a china cabinet that holds, instead of china, tinned peanuts, plastic bingo chips, fabric for kitchen curtains, a deck of cards and six rolls of Ganong peppermints. Stepping back into the kitchen, he sits at the table and takes out his cigarettes.

"Here," he says, holding the open package to Agnes.

She nods, take one and leans forward to light it as he cups the match in his hand. When she puts the cups of tea on the table he notices her nails, short and ragged, and the skin of her fingers, darkened creases.

"You work too hard."

"Pot calling the kettle black I'd say. So, how's business?"

"Same stuff, different day. I'll stay for the tea anyway but is there anything you need?"

"Actually yes. A bath brush. Reg dropped ours, cracked the handle right off at the bottom. Any blue?"

Ed nods, adds canned milk to his tea and stirs.

"And a white hairbrush and nailbrush for Lisa. That's it."

"How is Lisa, and the boys?"

"She's fine. Hardly see her what with her job and Modern Business College. Gordie's still out west, calls once in a while. And Dan's looking for work again. Laid off from the drydock."

"Too bad. Did you hear the news this morning? Some poor bugger jumped off the bridge. Now you tell me why would they go and build the nuthouse right there next to the falls?"

ેટ.

CARE OF THE INSANE
The beginnings of the Provincial Lunatic Asylum; a paper read before the New Brunswick Historical Society by Rev. C.T. Philips, February 23, 1904.

Less than a century ago, persons of unsound mind in most countries were treated worse than wild beasts. They were heavily manacled in cells and dungeons. The poisoned air not only prevented cure but hastened death.

A little more than a hundred years ago, the insane were irritated and tormented to gratify a morbid and vulgar curiosity. As a result of this treatment, many who were originally not beyond hope of recovery became permanently deranged. Those who were not deemed dangerous to public safety were left to roam about the country in a neglected and pitiful state.

And yet, I have found the grounds of the new asylum and the windows of the wings of this building look upon the Reversing Falls and the turbulent waters as they are rushed up through the gorge and won again, seething, boiling. They are swept together and then swept apart, as if by conflict. I have thought perhaps a mistake has been made in selecting a site for the asylum amidst such unrestful scenes, emblematic of reversing mind, now tossing forward, then flung hell-ward.

28.

Agnes can easily hear the chants from childhood — *You're gonna get sent across the bridge, to the nuthouse.* She never refers to the place but in her mind still calls it the nuthouse, that childhood name. A large stone building, bricks and mortar and huge boulders. Metal grates over the windows, bolts, locks, so very little wood to warm in the sun. Perched on the edge of a cliff, like some medieval fortress. Agnes would not be surprised to see heads impaled on wrought-iron gateposts, the ones she sees in her dreams. The asylum is situated at the end of a suspension bridge that spans Reversing Falls. Agnes used to imagine sentinels perched at the safe end of the bridge, waiting to walk the victims across to the other side. Children spoke of caged beds with covers made of wooden slats that locked over people, of lunatics screaming all day and all night, everyone naked and writhing and filthy.

Riding the bus across the bridge to visit her mother in the west side of the city, Agnes always holds her breath. Not a conscious gesture on her part, fear and habit. She looks at the advertisements above the pull-cord inside the bus, will not look out the windows at the churning brown water sullied with yellow foam from the mill. Agnes believes the bodies of people who die in the falls are never recovered. She argued this point with Lisa last year.

"They got that woman from the falls, eh, Mom," Lisa said.

Agnes put the bowls of pea soup on the table, didn't answer.

"They got her, Mom, it said so in the paper. Course there was no picture because she was probably all bashed up."

"They don't find them ..." Agnes whispered.

"Oh that's not true. They find the bodies. I mean, where would they go? They have to wash up somewheres."

੨

The Evening Telegraph, September 27, 1864

It is scarcely two years since the last addition was made to the buildings of the Asylum. As the structure stands now, it is the finest in the country. Its long façade of 300 feet, its two wings, each 150 feet long, and its central extension reaching back into an open court, stand out with most imposing effect. The monotony of the red brick is relieved by tasteful ornamentation of olive sandstone facings and trimmings. Graceful shade trees half conceal the front from view. Gravelled walks wind through flower beds luxuriant with bloom. A grassy terrace slopes down toward the river. A canary bird is trilling his carols in a window and the sound of a flute is heard in a distant angle. Perhaps a peal of laughter will ring forth at intervals, and if we listen closely, a low dreamy hum, like that which comes from a hive, will fall upon the ear. There is no shouting, no agonizing shriek, no sound of noisy wrangling, no wail of distress. There is a pleasing sense of quiet and retirement that startles us when we recall what is already forgotten — that 200 lunatics are confined within reach of the voice — that within this close corporation of weak intellects not one is master of his thoughts and actions. Here are the idiotic, the imbecile, the crazy, and the raving maniac, useless to themselves and a burden upon the world.

❧

Agnes pays for the brushes as Ed fastens his samples case and leaves. She goes upstairs to retrieve clothes from the hamper, then goes to the basement. Taking the washboard from underneath the laundry sink, she taps her foot, hoping the noise will frighten mice away. But there are no mice, only dirt and whirls of dust. The sink and the wringer washer, bathed in the light of a single overhead bulb, look squeezed into the corner of the basement. Elsewhere in the room stand piles of lumber, tools, wooden crates of fixtures salvaged from her husband's jobs, white marble doorknobs, brass letterslots. Her sons loved to look in the boxes when they were small boys, come running up the basement stairs to show her small treasures.

She runs hot water over the washboard, rubs a cloth against the pebbled grooves, plugs the sink and half fills it with cool water. From the pile of clothes beside the washer she finds what she is looking for, a small bundled towel, carries it to the sink and shakes loose her underwear, faded and worn. With the thick bar of yellow Sunlight soap she begins to wash the items, dipping them in the water and rubbing them until the water is white and foamy. No amount of scrubbing can remove the stains, reminders of her sudden, frequent starts of bleeding that no longer follow any pattern. When Lisa gets home the two women work together preparing supper. Lifting the lid on the potatoes, Agnes stirs them with a fork, careful not to scrape the light crust at the bottom of the pot. Lisa sets the table, humming under her breath a tune she heard on the radio. Both pause a moment hearing the car door slam and then Reg is in the kitchen. No greeting as he puts his thermos on the counter, washes his hands in the kitchen sink, wiping a wet fist across his mouth. As Agnes and Lisa get supper to the table, both try unsuccessfully to read his mood. He gets a beer from the fridge, opens it and sits at the table.

The women eat in silence, the muted sound of knives on plates. Reg's dinner remains untouched and he begins to read the front page of the newspaper.

Lisa finishes first, takes a piece of white bread, butters it and spreads a teaspoonful of sugar over it.

"Bad for your teeth," Reg says. "Better marry yourself a dentist. Morons will always throw money away on their teeth."

He pops his upper dentures out with his tongue and Agnes looks up to see them hanging, the false teeth perched on his lower lip for a moment before he pulls them in, clicking them loudly together.

"Bought and paid for," he says, taking another drink.

"Your supper …"

He pushes the plate with his elbow. "Christ, it's all dried up. I'm not eating that."

Agnes takes his plate and begins to clear the table, runs hot water in the sink to start the dishes. Lisa gets a dishcloth to help. Taking his beer and the paper, Reg goes to the living room, sits in his easy chair. Agnes is draining the sink, using steel wool to scrub the greasy film from the dishpan, when he returns, bangs his beer on the table. Pouring a cup of tea, Agnes comes to the table and sits, lights a cigarette, watching the match-flame lick the cardboard.

"Look at that bastard." Reg points to a picture of Pierre Trudeau on the front page of the paper. "Goddamned zombie was hiding in the woods while the rest of us fought for this country. We're being run by a bunch of no-good frogs. Look at that." His voice grows louder and Agnes leans slightly forward to see the Prime Minister surrounded by children waving small flags. She nods in agreement — with what, she doesn't know — and inhales deeply.

"Waving those red and white rags. I didn't fight under that thing … mickey liberal bastard. Shoot the bastard's what I'd do. Shoot the bastard."

Flecks of spittle coat the picture on the paper and Reg wipes his chin after he drains what's left in the beer bottle. Getting another from the fridge, he knocks over a bottle of green-tomato chow. Agnes fiddles with the book of matches, turning it around and around, then back in the other direction. Lisa goes to the living-room and Agnes can hear her reading something, the pages flipping.

"Mickeys put that bastard in power, having them big families like goddamned dogs, dragging everyone out to vote. White people don't have a chance in this country any more."

Reg continues for the next half hour, Agnes sitting and smoking, not saying anything, just nodding. Even her agreement seems inflammatory to him and he rails against her. Then suddenly he begins to sing, head thrown back and eyes closed. "This Old House", and his voice is beautiful, shows no sign of the drink, the tone rich and full. He sings the entire song and Agnes can hear the people next door moving about, not daring to bang on the wall. When he finishes he stands, pats her shoulder and goes upstairs.

Lisa comes and sits across from her mother, takes a cigarette to smoke more in companionship than from habit.

"He'll be sound asleep in a bit," Agnes whispers. Lisa notices the deepening furrows in her mother's face, the hair so grey now.

"I think I'll marry a mickey liberal frog dentist," she whispers and her mother grins, the lines softening.

"I'm gonna iron for a bit," Agnes says, picking up the beer bottle and her teacup.

"I'll clean up around the sink, Mom. I've got some sweaters to wash."

"We're out of Zero."

"I know, I got some on the way home."

Filling an old Windex bottle at the sink, Agnes goes to the ironing-board. The pile of clothes is small, a few blouses, some pillowcases and a dresser runner. She shakes a blouse and sprays it while waiting for the iron to heat. For as long as she can remember she has loved ironing, the hiss of hot metal on damp fabric, the smells of wind and cotton. Beginning on Lisa's blouse, moving about the buttons with perfect ease and grace, she wishes there were more items in the pile.

Her thoughts shift and travel with the moving iron. She thinks of the phone call today from her sister Mary, of Mary's fear that a second grandchild is on the way, out of wedlock. *Fallen girls.* She thinks of Mary's house, the geraniums in the window, the perpetual clutter of coffee mugs and ashtrays on the kitchen table, the steady stream of teenaged children coming and going.

It was to Mary's house that Agnes went when she left Reg, twice, when the boys were young, before Lisa was born. The first time was so long ago the memory is dim for her, pushed down beneath layers of years. She recalls hiding in Mary's basement while Reg hammered on the door, the sound of his shouting.

"Open this fucking door, I know she's in there."

"I'll call the cops," Mary yelled. Reg took a final kick to the door, then left, gravel spraying as he spun the car out of the driveway.

They stayed for four days, Agnes and the two small boys, all of them mixing with the chaos and dirt of the place. Then one morning Dan came to his mother in tears, a welt near his eye where Mary's son had hit him. For two nights Agnes didn't sleep at all, just sat at the kitchen table, smoking, watching the sky finally grow light. Then one morning she called Reg, hardly ten words between them, asking him to come get her. Mary stayed in the living-room, the heavy curtains closed while her children sat on the floor in the glow from the television.

Agnes remembers being startled by the day's brightness during the drive, the smell of Reg's workclothes. After they got home, she put both boys in the bath, washed their hair, dressed them in shorts and tee-shirts and sent them to play on the lawn with their toy cars. She could hear them through the screen door as she mixed ingredients for banana bread, mashing the soft brown fruit against the side of the bowl with a fork.

Lisa appears holding a rolled towel, squeezing it to take the moisture from her sweater.

"Do you want a tea, Mom?"

"That'd be nice."

Some water from the towel drips on the floor, and Lisa rubs it with her sock before going to the kitchen to put the kettle on.

WHATEVER ELSE MAY HAPPEN

The Salvation Army minister tells Agnes to remember the
happy times spent together.

"Pardon me?" Agnes says, the phrase she has been repeat-
ing to everyone in her path for the past two days.

Thinking he has not been heard, he raises his voice.

"Try to let your pleasant memories be a comfort to you.
Times you were together, doing things as a couple."

Agnes wonders if all ministers are fat, imagines they are.
Hard to resist the sweets pushed forward at every occasion,
baptismal parties, wedding rehearsal dinners, bazaars. She
can recall wrapping brown-sugar fudge for church sales
when the children were young, cutting the grainy squares
and folding waxed paper around them.

As a gesture of respect, the minister leaves his cigarettes
in the glovebox of his car during home visits. Agnes has
smoked three cigarettes since his arrival not long ago, and
he finally weakens, eyeing her package until she absent-

mindedly pushes it towards him and, as an afterthought, shoves the matches across the kitchen table.

Dan has gone to buy two white shirts, one for himself and one for his father, now in a hospital johnny-shirt at the morgue. He finds a parking place and enters the mall. The air inside is hot, unbearably so, in contrast to the clear November wind.

"Can I help you?"

There are three clerks in the men's clothing store, no other customers. The clerk approaching Dan is very thin, bad acne scars.

"I need two white shirts."

"This way."

Stepping past a rack of winter coats, the clerk leads Dan to the shirts, starts to pull packages from a unit of glass cubbyholes.

"You're about a fifteen?"

"I dunno."

"Hold on, I'll just grab my tape."

Not knowing where to look while the other man wraps the measuring tape around his neck, Dan stares up until the lights hurt his eyes and the pinpoint pattern on the ceiling tiles blurs.

"Yes, that's it. Now, do you want two the same? We have the plain white or this is very nice, see the fleck in the fabric, almost looks like linen squares."

"One plain and one like two sizes bigger but short-sleeved."

"Two sizes bigger? How do you mean?"

"Bigger than me. Whatever large would be, size large."

"Well, I don't think we even have short-sleeved shirts this time of year. Let me just look."

Dan wants out of the store now, can feel the sweat on the small of his back, starts to finger his wallet in his jacket pocket. The clerk kneels on the floor to pull a shirt from the bottom of a pile, scans the tag, then pushes himself upright, smiling.

"You're in luck. I've got this one in sixteen, on sale because it's old stock. That means no refund if it's not the right size, but you can get an exchange …"

Dan grabs the shirt from the clerk, walks to the counter and pulls the new bills from his wallet. Working on commission, the clerk still attempts niceties, talks about ties perhaps, but Dan says nothing, takes his change, shoves it in his pocket, hurries to the car.

The door is unlocked so he enters the kitchen, puts his keys on the table. He looks in the living-room and sees his mother asleep on the couch, covered in a quilt. The teapot is half-full and he pours a cup before turning the stove off. He adds two sugars and milk, stirring, the only sounds that of the refrigerator and clinking of his spoon against the side of the cup.

After drinking the tea, Dan opens his parcel, tears the cellophane wrapping from both shirts. He removes the pins, the plastic tabs at the top buttons, and throws them in the ashtray. For a moment he considers washing the garments but he wants to get everything to the funeral parlour this afternoon. He hangs his shirt over the back of a chair and goes to the dining-room, plugs in the iron and fills it with water. He presses his father's shirt, removes the creases as best he can, aware of the smell of sizing, what he calls *the new clothes smell*.

He goes upstairs quietly to his father's room, pulls back the curtain over the closet opening. He puts his father's only suit into a bag, adds shorts and socks. As an afterthought, he goes to the bathroom and takes some toiletries — his father's razor, bottle of Old Spice, toothbrush — puts them all in a shaving-kit he finds at the back of the bathroom closet and shoves this into the bag as well. Downstairs again, he gets shoes, a tin of brown polish, shoe brush, puts these in a shopping bag and leaves, shutting the door softly.

Dan has been to the funeral parlour once before, two years ago, when his cousin died in a car accident. Before going to the funeral he parked under the viaduct and smoked a joint. What he recalls of the event is the pink carpet, so thick and clean, and the wailing sound of his aunt sitting in the front pew, drowning out the minister's voice and, later, blending with the soloist's. The casket was closed and Dan saw no open caskets during that visit. In fact, he has never seen a corpse.

This afternoon it seems no detail escapes him. He stops in front of the signboard, black felt with white plastic letters. *Parlour One, Mrs. Ida Renfrew, Parlour Two, Mr. Randolph Sutton.* The lights are all on, even though it is the middle of the day. Dan notices lights everywhere — the large overhead frosted shades, wall lamps, table lamps. All have low-wattage bulbs, or maybe frosted pink bulbs that add to the glow of the hallway. There is no one at the desk at the end of the hallway so Dan keeps walking, looks into an empty lounge — huge green leather couches, marble ashtrays on stands, paintings of lakes with small brass light fixtures over each one.

Terrified of entering a parlour, he continues walking until he hears voices and the sound of china — a coffee room, he thinks. He heads down another hallway and sees bright lights from a room at the end. The door to the room is ajar and he pulls it open. There are two employees, both of them smoking, sitting in old wooden chairs, rungs missing. Both men are laughing softly, stop as the door opens. Not hired to greet the public, to offer condolences, these men wear casual clothes, work behind the scenes, vacuuming, polishing, moving. On a small table is a coffeemaker, the pot full, and one man stands.

"You're in the wrong place ..."

"I'm sorry. I'm ... I'm bringing the stuff for my father."

"Just go on back to the desk at the front," the man says, reaching for the wall phone. "G'won back there and I'll get someone to come out and meet you. Can you find your way?"

Dan nods and goes back down the hallway, his footsteps loud on the cement floor until he reaches the door.

Fighting to wake up, Agnes thinks that she hears a baby crying, that she is back in the cycle of mothering nights, up and down, up and down, sitting in the cold wooden rocker nursing one of the boys, willing herself to stay awake for fear she'll drop him. When her eyes open she sees the bottle of pills on the table beside her watch. It's three-thirty in the afternoon, and her thoughts scatter like a handful of marbles tossed down the basement stairs.

Lisa's phone call, not coming for the funeral, doesn't believe in funerals. I believe in one God, the Father Almighty, Maker of heaven and earth, And of all things visible and invisible. Gordie coming from Alberta, today or tomorrow. What day is today? Does Danny know to meet the flight? First time to see her granddaughters, Claire and Rebecca. Gordie's wife, Wanda Lee, saying no, they'd rather stay at the Delta hotel uptown, corporate rate. Time to start supper, he'll be home from work soon ...

The phone rings.

Think pleasant thoughts, the minister said. Sitting on the funeral-parlour couch, watching the boys move a flower arrangement, Agnes tries to move her thoughts beyond the papered walls of the room. She suspects Danny has been drinking, thinks he may have gone to the tavern with his brother after stopping at the hotel. Gordie's wife said she wanted to go shopping, to keep the children with her.

Danny won't go near the casket. Agnes watches him glance over every once in a while, then look away quickly. He fusses with the cards near the guestbook, sits in a chair near the door. Gordie talks almost nonstop to his brother, she can't catch the conversation, and Danny keeps nodding in agreement. They left the room earlier in the day, let her have time alone with him, but she could hear them whispering just outside the door.

A large part of her believes this is not him but, rather, a good likeness. She stares at his hands and takes their appearance as proof of this. Long ago he used to apologize about his hands, late at night, the two of them in bed, apologize for their roughness, stains no amount of scrubbing could remove. After work he would wash at the kitchen sink, a special tin of hand cleanser and a nailbrush, the water near scalding as he worked to lift the dirt. Though reddened from the assault, his fingers would never relinquish the markings of the workdays. The dead man's hands are immaculate, nails white, buffed to shining.

Agnes and her sons go to a small sitting-room on the second storey of the funeral home. This is the business level; a small team of young women in front of typewriters generate bills on handsome stationery. The director's office is here, with dark mahogany furniture, a china cabinet displaying urn selections replete with hidden lighting under each shelf. The sitting-room has a couch, a coffee-table, a bar fridge stocked with whole milk and coffee cream, and a trolley holding tea, coffee and thin dry biscuits.

There is a wall calendar, a scene of the Canadian Rockies for the month of November. Today is Thursday.

Agnes always bought groceries on Thursdays. Her husband picked her up and drove her to the grocery story. After dropping her off, he went to the hardware store, to chat with men he knew, while she did the shopping.

One particular Thursday, eight years after they'd married, he was walking down the aisle of the hardware store and banged into a wheelbarrow, part of a gardening promotion. There was a small selection of shrubs and plants waiting to be moved outdoors and he noticed a tag on one bush, a picture of purple flowers. He remembered his grandmother, her white hair in a tight bun, leaning to pile the fragrant boughs in his arms, the smell of lilacs through every room in the house, white lace curtains moving with the breeze.

He bought the lilac bush and drove to pick up his wife. Agnes was waiting inside the grocery-store door and he came to help hoist the brown paper bags, pile them into the back seat of the car.

Agnes was stubbing out her cigarette in the car's ashtray when he made a wrong turn, started driving in the opposite direction of home. He kept his eyes on the road ahead and she held her purse, watching his fingers tapping the steering wheel. He signalled and turned onto Quarry Road, braking smoothly round the curve. Agnes turned to watch the houses disappearing in the rear window, the bags of groceries packed together like cramped passengers across the width of the seat, and then the car stopped.

"Come on, get out."

Still clutching her purse, Agnes stepped out and closed the door, watched him open the trunk. He stood back and motioned for her to look inside. Leaning over, she saw a bush lying against his toolbox, roots wrapped in burlap.

"Lilacs," he said. "Purple. White ones have no smell to them."

Taking an empty tobacco tin from the trunk he walked to a pile of crushed stone. Bending on one knee, he scooped the dusty stone into the can. Agnes started to kneel beside him, uncertain of what to do, but he waved her away.

"I'll do it. Lime'll sweeten up the earth. That's good for lilacs," he said, rising when the can was full and dusting his hands on his work pants.

Agnes followed him to the car, stood near the open trunk and reached out to touch the burlap wrapping on the bush.

"Gotta get it wet, good and wet, get it in the ground," he said.

They planted the bush together, near the front door, out of the wind. Agnes remembers Gordie and Dan coming home from school that day to find Reg crouched, hands on his knees, while she directed the stream from a hose onto the freshly tamped soil. She doubts they recall the day at all. Nor would they remember the gesture, of their father laying a muddied hand on her arm, squeezing, or the look that passed between them before they noticed the boys.

> *Hear my prayer O Lord, and with thine ears consider my calling: hold not thy peace at my tears.*
>
> *For I am a stranger with thee: and a sojourner, as all my fathers were.*

O spare me a little, that I may recover my strength: before I go hence, and be no more seen.

— "The Burial of the Dead"
Book of Common Prayer

MY SOUL TO TAKE

Awful things I've seen in my days, awful things. Seen a grown man cry for me not giving him credit. I tell him, "What do you think I am, huh, a bank? You see me in some suit, asking how much you earn a month? If you got any assets? Pay as you go, or clear the hell out."

Seen a woman come here for the past ten years, bandaged up every time she comes, and I ask her what happened. "Fell down putting the dog out," she says. "Tripped on the back stairs — slipped on the ice." "The ice," I say and nod. "That ice is bad this year. Gonna be a late thaw, it is." Never mind, we know, her and me, loose lips and all that. Her nails are bit down to the quick, red and sore-looking. I try not to watch her hands when she counts the money onto the table. We don't talk a lot but she likes my cat.

June is the cat's name. She's a long-haired thing. Can't let her go outside — she'd take off — so I keep her indoors. Last year she sneaked out one afternoon and got such bad fleas I had to bath her in special stuff from the drugstore. Never saw a sorrier sight than that, poor old June, all draggled and soppy. Mean as spit she was — didn't think I was doing her any good dipping her in the sink, I guess — hid under the table for half the day, growling, but she finally come out, still damp but fluffed up a bit.

They put in a liquor store up the road, in the little strip mall. Used to be I was busier than a one-armed paper-hanger with crabs. Things have slowed down a bit but Sundays still bring the usual crowd, and the kids on Friday and Saturday nights. The kids — faces change every couple of years, one of them turns nineteen and can get the booze legal so that group falls off but, sure enough, the next lot slips into place. Sometimes I mix them up. "Aren't you Sonny's boy?" I say, and he says, "No, that's my cousin." I've seen a lot of grief over the years, not personally, mind you, but seen it in the faces of the men and women who come through my door. I keep no set hours: always open. Hell, I'm the jeezly bootlegger!

The new liquor store has a neon sign — "Open", "Closed". And displays — life-sized figures, a man in overalls, his head made of a nylon stocking, wearing a black fisherman's hat; a woman in a dress, red and white check like a picnic tablecloth — both figures seated on a big wooden swinging chair. Tee-shirts and jackets with beer crests hang from the ceiling, shopping carts are kept near the door. There is a rack full of brochures from liquor companies — recipes, designated driver promotions, fetal alcohol syndrome pamphlets. The flooring is rose-coloured stone tiles, fashionable but unforgiving to a dropped bottle. Never mind — a staff-person, uniformed, smiles and appears with broom and bucket, a little vacuum to retrieve the shards from under the rack.

Used to be there were two bootleggers in the area. One died a few years back, name of "Wiener" Bastrache, so called because he could swallow a whole hot dog in one go. Used to do this for an extra dollar whenever someone asked. By the time he went to the doctor, the lumps under his arm were like a clump of grapes. Dead in six months. Obituary read, "After a brief illness, passed away at home, predeceased by two brothers."

The other bootlegger, Weldon, still works. Buys his liquor every two weeks — goes to Saint John to get it. Drives a black van that used to belong to a funeral home. The van has big silver swirls on the side. The funeral-home owner took them from a casket damaged in transit and had them welded on by the local blacksmith.

The blacksmith lives in the rotting shed where he works; the rest of his extended family live in a series of old houses near the edge of a cliff, overlooking a small sheltered cove. They take his old-age cheque to the bank every month and cash it. Make a crooked "X" on the back, inform the teller their uncle can't write or read (a lie), keep his money. When the blacksmith sold his boat and lobster licence for thirty thousand dollars, cash, he buried the money; buried it while all the rest of them were in town buying Easter candy and stuffed rabbits. Sometimes the social worker sends the VON nurse to cut his toenails and she leaves a bottle of shampoo, for lice, she tells him, lice. That's why the whole family has them, because someone is always passing them on. He throws the foul-smelling liquid out the back door as soon as she leaves. The bottle breaks and the weeds turn yellow and die around the spot.

The bootlegger goes to the funeral home one afternoon to do some business, money in his pocket, a thick elastic band around the bills. He pays for a plain casket and also pays the fee to open and close the ground in a cemetery down the road where his parents are buried. He has no family living, doesn't want strangers involved when he dies. He does this shortly after Wiener Bastrache dies. In fact, he attended the funeral, heard the meanness in the voices of the few men who came to the service.

"Poor bastard couldn't even afford to bury hisself," they said.

While the funeral-parlour owner writes the receipt, Weldon stands at the window. He notices the van, the rust on the fenders.

"Better get that cleaned up," he says. "It looks bad."

"We're going to sell it."

"What it's worth?" he asks.

Weldon drives home, walks the three miles back, pays for the black van in cash, drives it home. For a while he considers removing the fancy scrollwork on the side — gets a crow-bar and tugs at one end — but the whole of the van's side starts to heave, so he decides to leave things alone. He polishes the curlicues with a can of Silvo after he mends the rust on the fenders.

I'm not ready to die yet, Jesus no, nowheres near ready. Better to be prepared, I say. Same as I get extra booze ahead for the holiday weekends, Easter, Thanksgiving, that sort of thing. Remembrance Day — now there's a day I do a lot of business, all the old vets like myself. From my place I can watch them marching up the road in the Remembrance Day parade; the Boy Scouts and the Girl Guides march too, carrying the flags. They all walk to the Legion for the wreath-laying. Not me, no. For a while I went to the Legion, but I'm not much of a joiner. Never have been. Rather keep my own company for the most part.

A lot of guys my age just want to talk about the war, except all they want to recall are the good times, make it sound like a big party, like we were on leave the whole time. Most of them heavy drinkers. They tell me, "Weldy, I drink to get feeling good." Who the hell am I to say different? I remember all the times, good and bad. No amount of drinking would make me forget. Not that I sit here and stew over it, but the facts are plain in my head, as if it happened just last week.

Basic training is where I first got noticed for the bronical trouble I have. Little girl up the drugstore, the druggist, looks about eighteen to me, she says "bronchial" right slow and on purpose so I might pick up and learn how to say it. I tell her, "Honey, we always called it 'bronical', that's what we called it." See, I had the whooping cough when I was but two years old, nearly died then. My mother had to stay up all night for two weeks with me, and when I was coughing so bad as to stop breathing, she'd throw me up towards the ceiling. She said on the way down I'd catch my breath, pull in some air. She did that for two weeks, and that's why I didn't die. Never had good wind, couldn't run much as a kid, but during training we had to put the masks on — gas masks — learn how they worked. Never could stand to have anything over my face or tight around my neck. Used to rip a little tear in the back of my sweaters so they wouldn't feel like they were closing off my throat. Well anyways, I couldn't put the mask on, felt like I was losing my breath. Ended up they made me peel fifty pounds of potatoes every single afternoon after that, until we left for overseas. As if peeling all them potatoes might change my mind about putting the mask on.

Everyone wonders if bootleggers drink. Hell, sure I drink. I'll have a beer — always have liked a beer. Not much for hard stuff, don't have the stomach for it. The thing is, though, I never took to it like some fellas, some girls for that matter. No, I could always have a few, then push away from the table. Some people aren't that way, have to drink till they pass out, come crawling on their belly for the next drink, same way as a baby needs a titty bottle.

Cops have never bothered me about my business. Only once did anyone ever give me a hard time about it. We had a new Baptist minister come to the church nearby. He come here one morning, sat right at the kitchen table. Talked nice to start with but I kept looking at my watch, so he got down to brass tacks. He said I was doing "Satan's work". I told him Satan was doing fine on his own, didn't need to hire the likes of me. Besides which, I was working for no one but myself. It was deer season and I still used to do some hunting then, so I got out my rifle to clean it. Got the oil and rags, set everything on the table. He high-tailed it straight out. I can still see him heading down the driveway, feet sinking in the mud, his shoe rubbers flapping in his hands either side of him, like black wings or something. Off he went and that was the end of that.

The bootlegger's home has blue vinyl siding. Not much in the way of neighbours — a few deserted summer homes with torn screen doors and sagging roofs. His house was once a summer home but he put the siding on, had a proper well and septic installed. He also bought a satellite dish. Dan was working for the company that sold the dishes and he drove to the bootlegger's to set it up. Weldon wanted a roof mount so Dan and his helper got on top of the house and did what was needed to prepare the site. Then they hoisted the dish and secured it while Weldon stood watching in the yard, yelling up encouragement. It was Dan's job to teach new owners how to use the remote. Weldon got them each a beer and they sat in the tiny living-room, the television zooming from channel to channel, all of them laughing when Dan stopped at the Playboy channel for a moment. Dan and Weldon took to each other, like some people do, with a sense of having known each other for a long time. Dan ended up telling the bootlegger about his younger sister, Lisa, "the smartest thing on two legs," he called her. They each had a second beer and then Dan and his helper headed back to the city, Dan promising to return a week later and make sure everything was operating properly.

Weldon tapes boxing from the television and sells the tapes — used to rent them but no one bothered returning them. When a big fight is on he makes ten tapes, sells them for twenty bucks apiece the next day. Stays up all night using his two VCRs to get the copies made.

Everyone at the drugstore knows him. Sometimes when his breathing is very bad, a lung infection, one of the staff will deliver his prescriptions. Last month he had pneumonia again, so the pharmacist packed up all his medications, an antibiotic, the solutions for his aerosol therapy machine, a bottle of ginger ale and cat food he called to order. She drove to his house, parked, knocked on the door.

Last autumn's leaves were frozen in the yard — the lawn had a pocked appearance. When he opened the door, a sudden wind moved past, pulling from the tiny house the stale

heated air, the smells of mentholated rub and stove oil. An-
noyed, the cat strutted to her litter box, squatted, kicked
gravel when she finished.

"Juney, Juney," he cooed to the cat, the sound of his voice
dry, the act of speaking starting a fit of coughing.

He had the aerosol machine on the kitchen table, small
glass medicine bottles lined up beside it. The plastic mask
and tubing were draped over the back of a wooden chair.
The pharmacist held the bag out to him.

"Come on in, come in." She stepped inside, pulled the door
shut behind her.

"Can you have a beer?" he asked.

"Oh no, I have to get back to work, Mr. Ramsey."

"Weldon, honey, call me Weldon. Mr. Ramsey was my fa-
ther and he's long gone. Well, how about you take a beer
with you?" He gestured to the large fridge beside the sink.
"Take one and you can have it when you get home, before
supper."

"Oh, no thanks. Um, how's your machine working?"

"Working good, honey. It's my lungs that are acting up.
Haven't been outta the house in two weeks."

He pointed to his pyjamas, old man pyjamas. She'd been
trying all that time not to look at him. They were grey flan-
nel, a paisley print, very wrinkled and baggy, though he
was not a small man. A tuft of white chest hair was vis-
ible at his neck, kinky and barbed as little lightning bolts.
One bedroom slipper had a large hole where his toe
showed through. He stuck his foot towards her.

"See here? I cut the hole on account of my gout."

When he started to laugh he coughed again, put both
hands on his chest and pushed as his face reddened. She
opened the bag and got a puffer out, ripped open the box
and shook the container, handing it to him. His hands

looked white, cold, and he nodded, put the puffer to his mouth, took two sprays. His coughing stopped.

"Are you okay?" she asked.

"Sure, honey, I'm okay. Listen, when is Tina working? I need to get her to set my watch again."

He held his wrist forth, a black watch they sold at the drugstore, LCD with a rooster that crowed.

"Can't get it fixed for the time change. Got the rooster crowing now at five in the morning."

"She's working tonight, I think. I'll check and call you when I get back to the store."

"Okay. You get going now. They don't pay you for doing house calls like doctors, do they?"

"No. Everything's in the bag here. You can pay next time you're by. We kept the receipt."

"That's good, honey. I'll be around next week, once the drugs kick in and get this chest cold outta me."

My life has been good. I suppose if it had been a lot worse I might want to die, but I don't though. That's why I keep all my drugs straight. When my breathing is good I just use the puffers. When it gets bad, I have to take the mask. Never thought I'd be able to use it, but the doc said, "The mask, Weldon, or I'll send you to hospital." I hate hospitals something desperate so I told him to leave me alone, that I'd see what I could do. The first few times were pretty bad, me shaking like a leaf, but I got the hang of it. You can get used to anything, if you have to, that is. Sometimes it's hard to hear the TV over the sound of the machine. I watch TV while I take the mask to make the time go faster, mostly the sports, but sometimes other stuff. Don't have the patience to watch a whole movie.

Last night I caught the end of a show about undertakers. Some kind of big meeting in the States, all these funeral fellas in black suits. They talked about different parts of the business. Then they had a big dance, all of them doing the twist in a ballroom, wearing those same suits. Must've been their wives too, all of them in black. Now, do you think they did that for a joke, wearing black, or just habit? Like some things you do for so long become habit. It's how a person is. Like me, I suppose — the bootlegger — that's who I am. Never mind I got the funeral home's old van. People see me going up the road in it and they all say, "There goes the bootlegger," because they know who I am.

AT ONE WITH NATURE

Wanda Lee and I went together for almost two years. I suppose that might not seem long but I'm pretty much a loner when you get right down to it. I met her at the bank where she worked. Had to go open a special account for the store and she helped me. I was living in a trailer with my brother Roy then, still am, as a matter of fact. She told me a lot about herself that first meeting, how she lived in an apartment downtown to be close to her job, how she liked spring and did I think the ice was moving kind of early that year.

Wanda Lee and her dates. She had this thing about the date when we first started *going steady*. Don't ask, because for the life of me I can't remember the moment, but she claims it was the first time I told her I loved her. Seems it was one of those private moments best not mentioned and in the middle of everything she must've said she loved me and I'm pretty sure I mumbled *same here*. Like I said, the details are fuzzy but after that she'd say stuff like "This is our two-month anniversary, this is our half-year anniversary," and so on.

We went to movies a lot in the beginning and I let her pick them — ones where the screen's mostly dark and you can't hear what anyone's saying. Looking back, I figure no one understood what was happening but they pretended, nodding and carrying on, which is just so much crap. But you see, back then I thought they got it and there was something wrong with me. It was a time when Wanda Lee was always at me to *better myself*. This included getting my hair cut downtown, ending up with me having to wear my ballhat every Jesus day for a month until it grew out. Plus there was a lot of correcting my talk.

"I'm gonna be drivin' out …"

"Driving. *Ing*. And not *out*. You don't drive out, you drive *to*."

She threw away a lot of my clothes but I only found this out later. I'd forget a sweater or something at her place and then the thing would just disappear. I thought Roy was taking my stuff but no, Wanda Lee finally fessed up. She said they were tacky. She made me go shopping with her and got all mad when I stood in the mall, my hands jammed in my jacket pockets, not agreeing to try on anything she picked out. We left with one shirt, purple. Last time I saw that shirt, Roy was using it to wipe the grease off his hands while he worked on his bike. I put it in the ragbag when it was still practically new.

In spite of all this, I did have a strong fondness for Wanda Lee and I tried as hard as I could to make things go right for us. A lot of time I thought about my father. I'd remember the three of us boys, morning time, lined up in the hall, all dying for a piss while our two sisters hogged the bathroom. There we were holding ourselves, leaping around in our longjohns, and the old man would come up the stairs, all grim-looking.

"You have to make allowances for women," he'd tell us, waving his huge hand to sweep us back into the bedroom. We'd go and dress, no one daring to talk back except Roy.

"Fuck 'em," Roy would mutter, pulling up the zipper on his jeans.

Roy says he won't get married until he finds a woman who can piss her name in the snow or skin a rabbit in less than a minute. Most of the time he's at the tavern but on Friday nights he goes to a dance and he usually brings a girl home. I used to spend Friday nights at Wanda Lee's but when I got back to the trailer Saturday mornings there was usually some girl grabbing a bite of toast, hair wrapped in a bath towel. Then Roy took her back to town and that was the last we'd see of her.

So anyway, I did make allowances for Wanda Lee. Part of my problem was just not knowing the right thing to say or do. I had no power of prediction when it came to that. Only after the wrong thing happened, only then would I know how stupid I'd been. The gift thing, for instance. Wanda Lee was big into presents, birthdays, Christmas and all. Even Valentine's and Easter. Well, when we first got together I *did* want to get her something nice. It was coming on to Christmas.

I work at Steve's Tackle Shop, have done since I was fifteen. Started there doing nights and weekends, didn't know shit really about fishing but I've always been a hard worker. The first year I mostly listened to the men who came there. I'd listen to the stories and watch them handle the gear and gaze at the cases of flies. Then one day Steve said he'd give me a deal on a fly rod, a great deal. I still didn't know nothing about fly-fishing then, only meat-fishing — what some people call bait-fishing. He took me out back after closing and we stood in the empty lot under the streetlight for must've been two hours with him teaching me how to cast. He said I had the touch and after that, well, every spare cent I made went on equipment and I started hitchhiking to the spots I heard people talk about, walking miles back in the woods to find places to fish.

All my thinking changed then, and this probably sounds crazy but I started to understand how fish think. I swear to God, it was like some sort of ESP you would see on TV, only not between two people ... between me and the fish. I'd know what they were thinking and lots of times when I was in the woods I'd talk to them, telling them it was no good, I knew where they were hiding.

Steve gave me some flies and when I had the money I bought what I could. I read a lot about fly-tying but didn't figure I could ever do it, seeing as I had my father's big hands.

"Ya should be a meat-cutter, hands like that there," my father would say to me when I was a kid.

I watched Steve tie flies; he had piano fingers, used to sit on a stool and lean over his work and in seconds make a Green Drake or a Quill Gordon appear. That first year fly-fishing I made a lot of mistakes, no doubt about that. Took me a long time to learn how to react after the trout would strike, how to move not too fast but fast enough. Just as well no one could see me cursing and laughing, they'd of figured I was half cut or crazy or both. Anyway, I finally got the hang of things and then I couldn't wait to get to work to tell my stories. Sure as shit, though, soon as I'd get to the good part Steve would start to laugh.

"What'd you get 'im on?" he'd say.

So I'd tell him and then he'd smile and nod at whoever else was listening.

"That's really my fish, boy," he'd say. "I tied that fly, so it was me brought the fish to the hook, see what I'm saying?"

When the season ended I'd saved up enough to buy a spare spool and line, a bobbin, hackle pliers, the essentials plus some hackles ... ones Steve said weren't fit to sell, let me have them for next to nothing. I figured it didn't matter because I'd ruin a fair bit of the stuff before I could tie anything decent. I was out in the trailer with Roy by then, and he'd come home pissed and sit at the kitchen table with me while I worked.

"Lose yer fucking eyesight doing that," he used to say before he fell asleep, leaning back in the chair with his mouth open, arms crossed on his chest.

By the time Wanda Lee and I got together, trout fishing was the most important thing in my life and I'd be lying to say it wasn't. Like I was saying, though, that first Christmas I wanted to get her something good. I tried to figure what to buy from looking around her place. I didn't know she had no interest in fishing. Sure, she'd never said she wanted to come with me and always seemed to have plenty to do with her friends while I was in the woods. She was big into crafts, that tole painted stuff, and it made sense to me that if she was good at finicky kind of things, she might be good at tying flies. So I bought Wanda Lee the best vice Steve sold, a rotary clamp one. I wrapped it, too, gave it to her on Christmas Eve after we went to midnight mass with her family.

It's not like I didn't spend a lot of money on her because I did, but Wanda Lee wasn't pleased. Not pleased at all. She cried and we had our first fight. She told me to take it back and get her something proper. Well, it didn't seem right to take it back so I just got a loan from my cousin and bought Wanda Lee a gold chain from People's at the Boxing Day sale. That pleased her a whole lot.

That next spring there was a big party for my parents' twenty-fifth anniversary, down at the Legion, and an uncle of mine came up from the States. He'd be my mother's brother, Albert, the only one ever made good. He owned a drugstore or part of one, something like that. He drove up in a white Lincoln which looked out of place with all the rusty Fords in the parking lot. Anyway, turned out he was a fly fisherman and he and I got talking, ended up getting pissed together and he invited me to come fishing with him in Cape Breton.

Before we left he came into the store and spent a lot of money. In fact, it might have been one of the biggest sales ever. I should have been glad but mostly I was embarrassed. He asked me to do all the driving, which was fine by me. That car felt like some sort of boat on foam, you'd of sworn there wasn't a hole in the road at all except I knew better. He knew where we were headed, gave all the directions.

Not long after we got to the river, I realized he didn't know near what he should have about fishing. Mostly he drank, then he'd fish for a little while, then drink more. For someone with all that money, he didn't seem very happy. In fact, he seemed kind of miserable — like he couldn't settle, he couldn't relax and let the fishing take over. He decided to have a rest so he laid back in the grass. I picked one of the flies I'd tied, a number 14 deer-hair bug, and clinched it to the leader. I'd seen a rise upstream in a brown pool behind a rock. First cast I hit the rock so I checked the hook to make sure it wasn't broke, but second cast was perfect. The fly sat there on top of the water for maybe five seconds and things were so quiet it was like slow motion. The brookie rose up, struck, I pulled.

I've got a picture in my wallet of me holding the fish. My uncle took the picture. He took a lot of pictures, come to think. Said he liked the little woman to see what he'd been up to. His wife mailed the photo to my mother. It's hard to see really good because the sun is behind me and I look all dark. I'm just as glad because, if you want to know the truth, I'm half crying in the picture and a second later I let that fish go.

The next winter things started to get worse for me and Wanda Lee. Her best friend had gotten married in the fall and Wanda Lee wouldn't let up talking about them. I got tired hearing all that stuff and her hinting all the time, buying that stupid Brides magazine and leaving it right on the couch or on back of the toilet. I don't like hinting around and besides, both of us were always strapped for cash and no way did I want to rush into getting married or anything.

One thing I will say — Wanda Lee and me always had a good time when we were alone. I figure you know what I'm trying to say here. So you can understand what a shock it was when I got there one Friday night and she was ripping open boxes from Sears — two lamps — and she dragged a chair and a stool into the bedroom and put the lamps either side of the bed. In a mood to fight, she was, telling me how her married friend said that her and her husband read in bed and accusing me of *keeping our relationship at its lowest level*. Her saying that hurt me, but the next Friday night I brought along two books, *The Metz Book of Hackle* and my new *Spawner*, and I sat there propped on a pillow and I read. Every once in a while Wanda Lee would set aside her book and look at mine and finally she snorted about *the intelligence of someone whose idea of reading is looking at pictures of feathers*.

I made one last-ditch effort that spring. Looking back, it seems sad to me, like when people have kids to try to keep the marriage together. Plain sad. I told Wanda Lee I'd take her back to the Bull Hole. Ready as I was for a fight, there was none in the works, and she listened to me when I told her what to wear. We set out just after dawn and drove her car to the end of the paving. We parked and started the hike.

The first two miles weren't bad and she seemed in good spirits. It's an old logging road but the mud was dried by then and the going was easy. After that, we had to take the turnoff and follow the trail. Over the years I've grown to know the path so well I could do it blindfolded. There are still a few markers, bits of torn cloth that I tied to the trees in earlier times so I wouldn't get lost.

Wanda Lee started grumbling soon after we were into the woods.

"Stay on the path," I told her.

"This is a path?" she kept saying, over and over.

Her face got scratched on a branch, which wasn't my fault but she made out like it was. I kept plugging on, hoping that once we crested the hill and she could see the pond at the bottom she'd brighten up. I remember the first time I saw it, how the water looked between the hills of spruce, so dark in the morning light they seemed black. It's one of the most beautiful spots to fish I know of. But no, sighting the water didn't do a thing for Wanda Lee. She'd gotten a foot stuck in a bit of bog and there was mud going down her boot. We made it to the edge of the pond and I started unpacking my gear.

"Where's the place to sit?" she asked.

"For Christ's sake, Wanda Lee, you don't sit when you fish," I said.

Soon as I said it I knew it was a mistake. The rest of the morning was a write-off, with her refusing to fish or even talk to me. Then I couldn't cast for shit and ended up losing a Muddler and a Mickey Finn. We left early and the next day we had a big fight. Wanda Lee told me she didn't want to hear anything about fishing for the rest of her natural life. I thought of telling her there was nothing natural about turning your back on nature but I kept my mouth shut. She said that if she didn't know better she'd think there was something wrong with me, that no one should have a hobby that took over their whole life.

I made a point never to mention fishing from then on. No doubt it was the turning-point for us and we were starting to drift apart, but I didn't really see it then, didn't want to. On the surface I tried to make out like everything was normal and okay, and we did our usual stuff. In secret, though, I was planning a trip to a spot I'd never been. I'd heard about it twice from different people. Sounded damn near impossible to get to but I had the maps out at night, studying them.

I told Wanda Lee I wouldn't be over one Friday night because I had business the next day. Lied to her for the first time, told her I had to help Roy with some stuff and we had to get an early start.

"Well, don't forget Bonnie's wedding on Sunday," she said.

Good thing she told me because I'd forgotten. Bonnie was Wanda Lee's *other* best friend. We were going to her wedding and Wanda Lee had made me get a new tie and had taken my suit to the cleaners and all. I said I'd pick her up Saturday night at eight. The wedding was in Truro but we were planning on driving up the night before and staying at a motel.

I wish I could explain what happened next but I can't. Some things can't be explained. I understand that now. No pictures, no amount of telling does any good. It's kind of like magic if you believe. You just have to take it on faith. I found the lake but it took me two hours longer than I'd figured. Before I got there I thought I was lost so I sat on a rock, was just about to light a smoke and then start back out when I heard a kingfisher. Put the cigarette in the pack and five minutes later I was at the water.

That day I caught trout like I never caught before. Fat! Those things were so fat it seemed like the skin was full to bursting. Never seen anything like it before or since. Felt like no one else had ever been there, me casting perfect every time. It got dark before I paid half a mind so I had to sleep there, which wasn't any trouble. I found a spot and laid down and next thing I knew it was morning, a Christly perfect morning. I stood up and started right into fishing again and was still there in the late afternoon when the search-and-rescue guys came along.

"How's it going?" one of them said to me.

"Fine as kind," I said.

I kept fishing and they left, headed over the next hill. Well yeah, it was me they were looking for, sent in by Wanda Lee after she couldn't get hold of me. Roy told her where he thought I'd gone. I didn't find any of this out until I got back to the trailer. I never got to talk to Wanda Lee because she hung up every time I called. I only went over there once, stood out on the lawn. I could see her because the curtains were opened. She was folding laundry and the TV was on. I suppose I could have gone up to the door and knocked but I didn't.

I thought about writing her a letter and telling how she should make allowances for things. I even started one, then ripped up the paper. I spent most of a month hanging around, not doing much. Roy tried to get me to come to a dance but I didn't feel like it. I didn't feel like much of anything. I had more than enough flies for the season, had been tying all winter and my boxes were full. Still, I thought it might help take my mind off things to tie a few so I got everything out of the closet and set up at the kitchen table.

Decided to have tea and a cigarette before starting so I put the kettle on. I was leaning near the door, blowing smoke through the screen. The rain was coming and you could hear it in the trees. "Don't you ever feel lonely out there in the woods by yourself?" Wanda Lee used to ask not long after we first met. And I used to tell her no, that I was never lonely. Only I don't know if that's true any more. I just don't know.

THE ACCUMULATION
OF SMALL ADVANTAGES

A thunderstorm occurred on June 2, 1953, forty miles south of Charlottesville, Virginia. Pushing a glass of lemonade against her swollen belly, Jessie Mitchell sat near the radio listening to the coronation. If her husband had been home he'd have hollered, more than likely something to the effect of "Turn that garbage off, Jessie! What the hell do we want to know about the Queen of England! Here we've no supper started, table's covered in clothes. Have you gone off your head?" Perhaps Jessie would have felt like agreeing to that; yes, she did feel off her head. For the fourth day now she had worn the same pink maternity dress. The dress bore perspiration stains, yellowish half-moons, but it was the biggest dress she owned, the one garment affording any semblance of comfort.

Jessie took what comfort she could while her husband, Albert, worked. Each year he took two weeks off work to drive to Canada to go fly-fishing. Otherwise, he kept long hours standing behind the pharmacy counter, mixing creams, counting pills into tiny bottles and typing directions with his index fingers, poke, poke, jab, his cigarette smouldering in the ashtray near his elbow. The ashtray had been a gift from a grateful customer, a souvenir she'd bought in Niagara Falls. The picture of the falls was all but obliterated by the residue of crushed cigarettes.

As unprepared as she was for labour, this being her first child and Jessie still in her eighth month, she was even less prepared for the thunderstorm. The royal procession was nearing the abbey when the clouds, a moment before white and high, turned black and seemed to press the earth, like a blanket wrapped too tightly around a feverish child. The sensation was the same, of hot breath under a blanket, stirring a film of moisture on the skin. Jessie barely had time to pull herself upright, turn off the radio, close the windows and pull the curtains, before the first bolt of lightning struck. She heard it, a searing hiss like cold tap-water poured into a hot fry-pan. The line ran jagged and hit the earth somewhere behind Johnson's barn, and seconds later came the thunder, so loud it blocked the sound Jessie made as the stream of amniotic fluid, warm but not scalding, like urine, ran down her legs and spread in a dark circle on the carpet.

The baby was christened Lenora and Jessie told of having to keep tiny flannel mittens on her infant daughter, how the moment Lenora's hands were freed she would flail and scratch her face or poke herself in the eye. What troubled Jessie most was that Lenora took no comfort from being held. The baby arched away, her legs pushing, face red from screaming. When Jessie put her in the crib she would continue to cry for a long time. Lenora had the worse case of cradle cap and diaper rash the neighbourhood women had

ever seen. They offered their advice — warmed olive oil mas-
saged into the scalp; a special soap for the diapers and three
rinses, two in hot water and a third in cold. Nothing seemed
to work and eventually Jessie kept to herself, made a point
to take Lenora out in the carriage when she knew all the
other women would be preparing supper. Albert took to
spending more and more time at work, coming home late,
and opening a tin of beans or making a sandwich with
canned corned beef, spreading mustard thickly on the store-
bought bread. Sometimes he would find Jessie sitting in the
rocking chair in the corner of the baby's room, crying softly,
while the baby slept in the crib. While Jessie rocked and
cried she wondered whether a second baby would be different, easier. Then her fear took over, the fear that another
baby would be just like Lenora, strange and difficult, or possibly even worse.

When she was seven years old, Lenora would give her ten-
cent weekly allowance to an older cousin in exchange for
the opportunity to pick his sunburned back. He would sit
on the padded footstool in the cool, darkened living-room,
his tee-shirt folded on his knees, breezes blowing though the
lace curtains and making him shiver. Behind him, Lenora
would put her face so close to his back that he could feel
her breath, and then her fingers working to lift the dry and
hardened skin. She liked to take off as large a piece as possible at one time, pry the top margin of flesh free and then
lift, lift at the edges until a whole sheet of skin was removed.
Sometimes he would bleed, light pinpricks of blood coming
to the surface, then swelling to join together, a Rorschach
inkblot card come alive. He never complained, but he set a
time limit. Occasionally he'd glance at his watch.

"Three minutes left," he'd say and, a moment later, "I want the dime as soon as you're done."

Then she would hurry, leaving the difficult area near his spine and concentrating on his shoulders, where the smaller whitish scales, lizard-like, were shiny as mica and lifted with almost no prompting. When the time ended he'd put on his tee-shirt and leave the house, grab his bike and head for the river, where his friends were waiting for him. Lenora would roll the accumulated skin into a ball, like the tin-foil ball she saved from the linings of Juicy Fruit gum wrappers. One piece of skin pushed onto another, onto another, until there was a small whitish-brown ball the size of a marble. Often she dropped it into one of the potted spider plants.

Cleaning house, her mother would frequently come upon a pile of skin or nail shavings near a chair and know that Lenora had been there, reading or watching television. Her hands were never still; she dug at her nails, splitting them, tearing off little shreds, going at them incessantly. When she exhausted the possibilities with her fingernails, Lenora attacked her feet and twice had to be treated by Dr. Bailiss for ingrown nails on her big toes.

She was not a child given to *fits of kindness*, a saying often called forth when people spoke of Jessie. If the local women could have called Lenora's parentage into question they would have. Easier to believe the girl had been a foundling or some such thing, but no, there she was, spawn of Jessie and Albert plain as day. Everyone had seen Jessie swelled up like a grapefruit, and the child had her father's beaky nose and coarse eyebrows. A freak of nature that she should be such a contrary thing, so given to tantrums, throwing herself flat on her back in the shoe store until Jessie relented and bought the black patent leathers for the first day of school, never mind every other child in town would be in brown Oxfords.

As much as Jessie feared the thunderstorms that inevitably came each summer, Lenora loved them. She once ran into the yard with her father's fly rod, snapping the pieces in place as Jessie screamed from behind the screen door, "You'll die, you'll die," but Lenora didn't die. She ran about the thick green lawn in her bare feet, the hot rain soaking her clothes to her lean frame, waving the eight-foot rod back and forth, it snapping like a drunken metronome. For whatever reason, lightning did not strike the child.

Jessie had hoped the child might outgrow her willfulness, her oddness, but she didn't. The fear of having a second child made Jessie avoid Albert, move her head when he ducked to kiss her sometimes, after Lenora was in bed and they sat watching television. She turned away from him on those nights when his hand moved in the dark and rested on her arm, kneading, pleading. She yawned and talked about washing curtains, and curled in upon herself, wrapped up in a circle of aching want and fear, and counted repeatedly to one hundred until she fell asleep.

Lenora's father died running across the road one evening at dusk. He'd been kept late at work, having to mix a Brompton cocktail for poor Mrs. Miller, whose bowel was being eaten by cancer. The cocktail had all manner of narcotic, enough to kill a horse, as they say, but Lenora's father laboured to give the mixture a pleasant taste. He mixed peppermint water, filtered it, filtered it a second time, then added it slowly to the amber bottle, pausing to mix with a glass rod after each addition. By the time he got the label typed the sun was at a crazy angle, bouncing off chrome and nickel and fighting its own dying reflection in the storefront windows. Little wonder he was struck down, taking such a chance as he did, people said. No one, not even Lenora's mother or Lenora, ever dreamed of the times he'd gazed at that same street while he worked, gazed in fact at the very spot where he would be struck and killed; nobody ever guessed how he imagined the feel of the impact, the deafening sound of rubber on pavement, metal on bone, and then the silence while life ended. He'd made sure all things were in order the previous year so as not to raise suspicion. The well was working smoothly, the roof had been done three years before, the mortgage could be retired by selling his interest in the drugstore to his partner, who would eagerly buy. The insurance was paid up and there was a small bundle put aside to allow Lenora four good years of university, even if she chose to move far from home.

Far from home was exactly where Lenora chose to go, in pursuit of a young man she began dating prior to high school graduation. Byron Cummings felt puzzled by her advances and for weeks couldn't bring himself to admit that yes indeed, she was coming on to him. No female had ever shown any romantic interest in Byron, much less sexual interest, but there she was, leaning against his locker, asking about seat sales for the latest Shakespeare production the school was presenting. One noon-time she came and sat across from him in the cafeteria, the table near the front; the steam from the vegetables, greying broccoli and carrot buttons, drove most students as far away as possible. He had a calculus book propped on the sugar dispenser and was reading as she sat down. "Hi," she said.

He shrugged, not knowing any better, not replying or attempting conversation.

"Well, tell me what you think about the games between Fischer and that Russian," she said.

Bobby Fischer. Yes, a girl who knew of Bobby Fischer and mentioned him as nonchalantly as the other girls wearing orange and green plastic jewellery might speak of nail polish or movie stars. He gazed at her as she took the tiniest bite of her egg-salad sandwich, watched as the tip of her pink tongue came just to the edge of her lip to catch a drop of mayonnaise, and fell completely in love. He would often think of this moment, how his chest seemed to swell and pull his shoulders back into the chair, how his breath seemed to go through his body to his hands and fingers, and his eyes felt as if he'd just finished crying for a very long time. He knew nothing about Lenora, in fact, he wasn't even certain of her name at that moment. Leanne? Leanette? But although he knew nothing of her, Lenora knew a fair bit about Byron.

She wanted to marry a dentist. Gold-digging, the girls would call this. Going to university to get your MRS. degree. Lenora had volunteered to work on the high school yearbook, the write-ups committee. She had read Byron's graduation write-up two weeks ago, submitted typed when all the rest were hand-written on loose-leaf.

> *Per ardua ad astra.*
>   Byron came to high school three years ago
> from Westfield and has been a whirlwind of
> activity ever since. His interests have included
> bowling, reading, typing and playing chess. He
> is a member of Inter-school Christian
> Fellowship and treasurer of the drama society.
> He is also chairman of the chess club. Next year
> Byron intends to begin his science degree at
> Loma Linda en route to dentistry.

Lenora's thoughts on dentistry ran like this: Dentists were wealthy. Dentists were clean and had summer homes and convertible sports cars. Dentists played tennis and had lean tanned legs to go with white shorts. Dentists' wives had lovely teeth. Dentists always had fresh mouths, no cold sores, no chapped lips, no beard stubble or cracked teeth. No, just cool minty mouths with perfect white teeth.

Lenora followed Byron to California. By the time he had finished two years of science and had been accepted into the dentistry faculty, she had entered her third year of a liberal arts program with no declared major. She vacillated between history and sociology and for a brief time considered archaeology, all that lovely digging and picking and brushing away flecks of time with little instruments and special vacuums. Archaeology seemed quite similar to dentistry, thought Lenora, as she sat in the darkened university classroom watching a documentary about a dig in Australia.

During her years at university in California, Lenora paid little heed to Jessie. She often failed to acknowledge the parcels her mother sent, boxes packed with soap, lavender sachets, cans of cocoa, covered elastics for her hair. She gave these things to the others in residence. The summer of her third year away, she took a job as a library assistant at the university. The pay was very good and Byron was taking a summer course and doing his clinical service in the dental clinic on campus. They found an apartment to share that fall and Lenora chose to keep her job at the library, take some time away from her courses to decide what she truly wanted to do. They announced their engagement in December and were married back home the following May.

After Byron graduated, they moved to Davis. Property values were still affordable but escalating, a sound investment. Lots of young families. Jessie called them once a month, for a while fantasized about grandchildren. She dreamed of a child, an infant, as unlike Lenora as she could conjure. A warm small body that would lean into her soothing words and take the shape of her arms and soft chest. She hoped for a baby that would be left in her care for extended periods of time, that she could take to the park in a carriage and hold under the elm trees. Old couples she knew, out walking their dogs, would stop and peer down at her grandchild's face nestled among the knitted blankets and they would coo and feel envy.

Lenora and Byron had no children. Suddenly their twenties vanished, and just as quickly their thirties. Some things unfolded as Lenora had expected, others not. She had a sports car and took tennis lessons. Byron did not like tennis, refused to come to lessons, and when he tried on the white shorts Lenora had bought him they both agreed that it was amazing to see such white flesh in California. He worked long hours and had a loyal following of patients. They spoke of his compassion and delicate touch. Lenora had a brief affair with a tennis instructor, Jim, but after a time felt a growing revulsion for his coarse language and his task-oriented approach to love-making. On television late one night — she was often insomniac — she watched a re-run, *The Fuller Brush Girl* with Lucille Ball. She laughed so much that Byron woke up, came out of the bedroom mussed with sleep to ask what was wrong. After he went back to bed she turned off the television and wept, guilt arriving with sudden piercing intensity, settling beneath her ribs.

A week later the call came from one of her mother's neighbours. Seemed Jessie was ill, did she know? They didn't want to interfere but it might be time for a trip home, to see for herself. Lenora went alone; Byron was presenting a paper at a conference in San Francisco.

Jessie was ill, no doubt about that. Twice Lenora found her sitting at the kitchen table, looking into the old View-Master Lenora had owned as a child. The stack of reels was pushed to the back of the table — "White Sands National Monument, New Mexico", "The Seven Wonders of the World", "Boulder Dam Powerhouse Tour". There was no reel in the View-Master, but Jessie had it pushed so hard into her face that when she removed it her eyes were ringed in red.

"What are you looking at?"

"It's a stage in there. Little black curtains pulled back on the sides. Sometimes I see a foot start out but something always comes and scares them away. Look Lenora, look for yourself."

And Lenora did look. Took the toy from her mother and held it gently, tried to focus. One blank square of white light which changed to a darker white when she shifted position, moving away from the brightness of the table lamp. There were bits of black at each margin, metal parts inside the workings. A blank View-Master was all it was.

The doctor talked about Alzheimer's, any history of senility, too much time alone, too little to do, any family history of manic depression or schizophrenia. Caregivers, institutions.

Lenora had been back in Davis less than a year when the call came to return home, this time from the doctor. *Sunny Vale Rest Home*. The white wooden sign had black-painted letters in fancy script. Marigolds, their odour pungent, grew in orderly patterns around the base of the sign, and the long paved driveway led to visitors' parking.

The weather was unseasonably mild. Lenora wore an Albert Nippon suit, skirt and short jacket, red with white polka dots. She could feel the sweat behind her knees as soon as she stepped from the taxi she'd taken from the airport. The receptionist wore street clothes, no white jackets, and there were patients everywhere, furrowed and shuffling but well dressed and clean. No sudden bursts of laughter but what could you expect? Following directions, Lenora found her mother's room, a little suite actually, coffee table, beige lamp, a love seat, a wooden bed with side rails, one up and one down. A nurse came in and startled her.

"Oh, are you Jessie's daughter?"

"Yes."

"Follow me. We're just giving your mother a bath. Down here."

The nurse was talking over her shoulder as they went, stopping at a cupboard to pick up a stack of white towels, pushing a mop and bucket to the side of the hallway.

"She came in with a fair number of sores, groin mostly but we've got them pretty much cleaned up ... wool pad under the mattress cover ... not unusual ... had her morning meds and an extra dose ... might not recognize you ..."

The nurse stopped in front of a door, knocked once and entered, Lenora trailing a few steps behind. The sound of running water stopped as they rounded a curtain and Lenora saw Jessie, strapped into a chair that looked like a child's circus ride. She was naked and shivering though the room was very warm, possibly near eighty degrees. Another woman, Lenora assumed she was a nurse, was patting her mother's shoulder, talking in a low voice. She looked up and smiled at Lenora but Jessie kept her gaze on her incredibly small lap, her legs shrunken like old tree branches. A bonsai tree, Lenora thought, looking at the twisted wrinkled limbs, the flesh so loose.

"Won't let us bathe her, no how no where ... we tried all the other routes. We only do this once a week. No choice with the sores."

The nurse pushed a button and the chair holding Jessie began to rise in the air. She fought the restraints and bit her lower lip. The chair rose over the invalid bath; it looked like a large version of the old wringer washer tub Jessie had once used for doing laundry. Another button and the chair moved over the tub and began to lower slowly until the water came over Jessie's feet, up to her knees, along her lap to the empty rolls of flesh that were her belly. Lenora watched her mother's arms push against the white restraints, and then the water was chest-high and a nurse was reaching in with a sponge, moving an antiseptic-smelling foam over the old woman's shoulders.

Lenora had not moved. Jessie looked up suddenly and stared at her daughter, mouthed a word in silence — *thunder* — then closed her eyes and pulled her chin to her chest.

EIGHT DOWN

Gordie threw up on our wedding night. You might say that was a catharsis of sorts — that's a new word I just learned. I've learned a lot of new words from doing crossword puzzles. Oh, and the Lexicon on Friday nights in the newspaper. Some day I expect to win the five-hundred-dollar prize for that. I put my entry in the mailbox every Saturday, in front of the grocery store.

He had been drinking since noon the day of our wedding, most likely nerves. I knew he was half cut but I didn't let on. Everyone was pretty nice about it except Bernice, my cousin's wife, who from the word go has been a bitch. Shrew, termagant.

That's the sad part about living so far from home. You kind of have to take what you can get in the way of friends. Back home I had some really good friends, women who would never let me down, the kind I could tell stuff to and not worry about it being spread around. The money is good out here, though. That's why everyone comes. Don't let them tell you any different. The air is so dry I get nosebleeds all the time, have to have a humidifier running and put a special spray up my nose. Winter hits like a ton of bricks and doesn't let up for ages. All of us from the east coast, Gordie included, just roll our eyes when locals talk about the mountains, oh the mountains this and the mountains that. Who gives a damn? Nothing can compare to being close to the water. Someday we'll probably move back east, when we have enough money saved up.

We honeymooned at Howard Johnson's, right there next to the highway. Not a hell of a lot in the way of scenery, but we both had to be back to work the following Monday. The sad part is that I got a bad stain on the sleeve of the peignoir I was wearing. No matter what, that stain would not come out. It took me half an hour to clean up the mess in the toilet and the sink while Gordie slept it off. You see, I wanted to leave the room clean. In my opinion, people who leave a mess, the type who steal hotel towels and such, are nothing better than trash. Deviants, malefactors, subversives. A year later I tried bleach on the peignoir and ruined the thing. Annihilated, extirpated.

I've learned all these words and believe me, I'm still gathering plenty, but I never get to use them in conversation. I tried for a while. Then one night we were at Bernice and Tom's new modular home. He's my first cousin on my mother's side and works with Gordie. We were playing *Scrabble* and I used the word *grimace* only I pronounced it like grime and ace and Bernice corrected me. She says my name wrong, puts the stress on Wanda but the strong part is supposed to be Lee, not Wanda. It's supposed to be Wanda LEE, not WANDA Lee. It's not like those cake things, Sara Lee. I was miffed but I let it pass and we kept playing, eating peanuts and drinking beer in Blue Jays mugs. After a while she made us take the tour. Gordie made a kind of crude comment about the mirrored closet doors in the bedroom, and he and Bernice snorted and tittered over that the rest of the way through the two bathrooms, the den and the laundry room. Poor Tom just shrugged. He shrugs a whole lot, so much you'd swear there were little invisible strings between his ears and his shoulders that someone yanked, like on those marionettes.

Well, it's rude, plain ignorant, to correct someone's speech in front of other people. Not that Bernice cared. She kept pushing and pushing, telling me all night not to go grime acing on her, pulling out the words. Gordon laughed a lot too, and said I should get off my high horse and speak plain English like the rest of them. Never mind that he calls Cape Breton "*Cape Britain*". To make a long story short, that night was the end of my trying to use my improved vocabulary. After that I kept it to myself, private business. Secreted, furtive, occult.

Bernice planned an anniversary party for herself, which is bad enough, but she planned it months in advance too. As soon as the Christmas stuff was packed away she got to it, calling us all with menu ideas, roping us in to help with decorations and the like. It was their tenth anniversary, which seemed no big deal to me but she said ten years was damned good in this day and age.

She invited people our age and some younger, forty of us all told. She had a big surprise planned for Tom. A stripper was coming. All of us women knew but she made us swear not to tell the men.

I got there early, as I was supposed to be part of the decorating crew. Bernice was busy fussing with bowls of pickles, putting crackers around the cheeseball. There was a punchbowl with ice-cubes shaped like triangles, coloured with green food colouring, except the little things melted into green blobs. This was on account of the ginger ale being too warm when she added it.

"Someone snot in the punchbowl?" asked Cheryl, Bernice's so-called best friend.

"Eat shit," Bernice replied.

The phone started ringing but Bernice had her hands in the sink, picking the guts out of shrimp.

"Get that, someone get that," she said.

So I got it. The stripper was calling to say she was sick and would be sending a replacement from the agency. Changeling, facsimile, likeness. I hung up and told Bernice, who had a fit and tried to call back, getting shrimp guts on the receiver and everything, but there was just an answering machine on. The thing was, Bernice had asked for a theme stripper to go with the party — yellow ribbons, preferably a yellow suit, and she had specifically asked the stripper to tie a yellow ribbon on Tom's head — he's going bald. I could just see him shrugging with the stripper's boobs in his face and all.

Not much could be done so we just kept on decorating, lots of balloons and crepe paper and a big gold banner that spelled *Happy Anniversary*. I pictured Bernice buying all the stuff at The Party Place, piling it in the cart and no doubt yakking on to some poor cashier about the whole event. Bernice thinks everyone in the world is interested in her life, the boring details. She is so far off the mark it doesn't bear commenting on. My mother would say she's a classic case of someone who knows the price of everything but the value of nothing.

People started coming and then there were drinks to pour, plates to pass out, casseroles to be put in the oven to warm.

The punch had turned a pale brown by then but no one seemed to care, and someone dumped a mickey of gin into the bowl as well. We played charades and some of the people danced but then the men got fed up and went to the den to play darts. Next year it would be pool, Bernice promised. We'd all had to chip in twenty dollars for the anniversary gift, which turned out to be nothing more than cash to put towards that pool table.

The doorbell rang about an hour later. Bernice ran to get it and we all kind of crowded forward. You wouldn't really have known it was a stripper. She had a perm all fluffed out, big hair like a country singer or the people you see at Tim Horton's. It was blonde, looked like a drugstore dye. She wore a black woollen coat, but that made sense because it was still cold at night, and she was carrying a little ghetto-blaster. She put that on the floor as soon as we opened the door.

"I need five bucks more for the cab," she said.

The driver blasted his horn and Bernice ran for her purse, pulled out a new five-dollar bill and handed it to the stripper. I noticed the stripper's nails, very long, probably acrylic tips, painted dark red. She sure took her time coming back up the driveway.

Bernice grabbed her right fast and pulled her down the hallway to the bathroom. That was our cue to get the men ready. I went to the den. The door was shut and when I opened it the first thing I saw was a forty of rye on the desk.

"We're in the middle of a game."

"Give us a break."

"Fuck off, why don't ya?"

It took some work to get them all into the living-room, and Gordon was reeking of booze. They took their places on the L-shaped couch and on card-table chairs Bernice had borrowed from her neighbours. They were grumbling a lot.

Then Bernice came down the hall, all flushed and set down the ghetto blaster. The men were talking to each other, no one paying her any mind, so she stood on a footstool and clapped her hands.

"Everyone! Everyone! I want to say thank you to all of you for coming and honey, I hope the next ten years are as much fun as these first ten. This here is my special little present. Happy anniversary!"

She jumped down and pushed play on the blaster. All we heard for a while was static. Bernice yelled, "NOW!" and the bathroom door opened.

The stripper was wearing a red and white striped top which made her look like a candy cane. The red satin shorts were riding high and her legs had that bumpy orange-peel skin that the magazines are always telling you how to eliminate. She'd put on red stiletto heels and had a hard time walking on the shag carpet in the hallway, though the lower-pile carpet in the living-room didn't seem to trouble her so much. All the women were in a big clump, like an octopus with about a hundred arms. The men started hooting, slapping their knees, and one guy stood up and did some pelvic thrusts. Bernice pointed to Tom and the stripper went over and stood in front of him as the music started, feeble, no bass to speak of. Bernice turned it up but it sounded even worse so she turned it down again.

Lord knows I'm no expert when it comes to stripping. I have never done it, never intend to do it. Some women I know put on a show for their husbands sometimes, dancing and taking bits off, candles in the room and music. Number one, I would just not do it but say I did; number two, Gordon would think I was ready for the nuthouse.

For the first minute all she did was dance, hardly moving at all, little steps to one side, then the other. After a bit she pulled her top over her head, which lifted her hair up a lot and you could see all the black roots. There was no bra or any of those dangling things I expected a stripper to wear. She must've sewn Velcro down the back of the shorts, though, because she just whipped them off in one tug and tossed them on the hearth. Nothing underneath. Nothing. The song ended then. One guy jumped up and started clapping and she took that opportunity to plunk herself down on the couch in the empty spot, wiping her forehead like it had been a hard job.

"Someone wanna get me a beer?" she asked.

Bernice's face was all twisted in a laughing-crying look and she grabbed a handful of yellow party napkins from the coffee table. She stood in front of the stripper and held out the napkins.

"Don't you sit your bare arse on my new couch," she said.

"Oh for Christ's sake," the stripper said, standing up. "Well, can I have a beer or what?"

"I wouldn't give you a goddamned glass of water," Bernice said, and then she started crying and ran out of the room. Tom shrugged and headed off after her. I ended up calling a cab for the stripper and paying her the other forty bucks Bernice owed. The party kind of flopped after that and people started leaving.

When we got home Gordie threw up in the driveway. He could never mix his liquor and I knew he'd be in a bad way the next morning. I stayed up, sat at the kitchen table drinking a pot of tea, reading all the classified ads in the paper and saving the crossword for last — my consolation. Solace, respite, comfort.

COME FROM AWAY

Oprah says the reason we want to get reunited with old boy-friends is that we have unresolved feelings of rejection. I was going to write to Oprah but figured I'd just get some form letter back in the mail from a Harpo employee, *Dear Wanda Lee, thank you for your interest in the show but unfortunately we get so much mail ...* It's too bad because viewers like me, ones who watch her faithfully, we're the ones she should listen to. I'd tell her three things. One — even though you're skinny now, fit and trim anyway, don't be wearing those tight outfits. It always makes a person look big, having on something pulling at the waist or all stretched round the hips. I should know. I also understand why women do it. Because of the rush of getting into a size eight. Well it's not worth it. Wear the ten, wear the twelve. I mean, even those skinny models would look a little chunky if you stuffed them into too-small sizes, like a sausage ready to split its skin.

Two — stop touching people. You'd think Oprah would know better than to go and invade people's personal space, what with her history of the sexual abuse and all. Some days it looks like she's just plain tired and who can blame her, getting up at four in the morning to go to that club and work out? Speaking of which, I thought that was very brave going on TV with no make-up and her hair not done, that time she showed us where she worked out and then took us backstage while those two guys did her hair and make-up. Anyway, there is no good reason to be holding onto people's arms or shoulders while they're talking into the microphone. Just stand there and let them talk. Plus try to learn how to stand nice, not all the weight on one side. I don't know, maybe her feet hurt. Some of those shoes look pretty baked, not the kind of thing you want to run around a studio in. She'd be a lot better off in flats or just a low heel. Back to the weight thing too, flat shoes won't make her look dumpy as long as the clothes aren't tight, and that's a fact.

Three — stop talking about Stedman and marry him. He seems a kind and decent person and he must have a powerful sense of himself to stand by her all the time she was working it out. Plus now he probably only gets to eat what Rosie cooks. You can tell there's a lot goes on with the whole Stedman issue, and if you notice, she's been mentioning him a whole lot more often lately. That is just so telling. I mean, you know straight off when someone keeps bringing a certain person into a conversation every single chance they get, never mind the whole talk had nothing to do with that person in the first place, know what I mean?

There was this famous guy on the show last week. I didn't catch his name because the power was out so I missed half of it, but he said that Oprah was a role model to millions of women and that she had proved baggage does not control destiny. Isn't that cool? Made me think like you don't have to take the luggage on the trip. I loved that. You could tell she did too because for once she was quiet. If I was going to tell her four things, which I wouldn't, I would say don't talk so much. Yes it's a talk-show and you're the talk-show hostess, but let those people have their say, don't be cutting them off all the time with your stories or thinking you can quick fill in how their adventure ends. But, like I said, I'm not writing to Oprah because I figure it would plain be a waste of time.

I've been doing a lot of thinking about that unresolved rejection. My best friend Bonnie ran into one of her old boyfriends one day last week, right at the grocery store of all places. She wrote and told me. We keep in close touch by letter. She said that it was dead embarrassing, that she had both the kids with her, cart full of sugar cereal and bologna, family food. Out of the blue he appears, down by the deli section. He told her he'd just moved into the condos near the new subdivision. Said she should bring her husband over and play *Pictionary* with him and his girlfriend. Bonnie told me all he had was a little wire basket holding some pate and cheeses. Honest to God. Bonnie said it was kind of a relief to finally run into him, after all those years of dreading coming face to face with him somewhere downtown. She said she wished she could bang into an old lover every Friday for the next two weeks, get it all out of the way and then it would all be over. Only three old boyfriends, can you believe that? Not that she's a prude — we discuss some delicate topics in our letters and Bonnie is well informed when it comes to sex — she just lacked certain opportunities.

I don't suppose I'd have quite so many ex-boyfriends if I hadn't gone to Fort McMurray that summer I was seventeen. Hardly anyone even knows where the place is now. Some people are so stupid, you'd swear they never read the paper. For a quick refresher, McMurray is in Alberta, way north of Edmonton, a boom town because of the tar sands, oil money. Back in the seventies, early eighties, half the Maritimes went there looking for work. Half of Ontario too, come to think of it. Everyone that went to McMurray was young, some with no skills but a lot of fellows fresh out of trades school. The average age of that town was twenty-three and the ratio of men to women was ten to one. I wish I knew the number of yellow Corvettes compared to the population there because it was amazing. There was always a party, the bars were always full. I should know, I was a waitress back then. Lied about my age on the application form, but not like they would have checked it out. You could have said you worked at the White House cleaning toilets and they'd have just said, "Uh-huh," the place was so desperate to get some female help.

My cousin Carl had gone out after his pipe-fitting course. When he'd been there for six months he sent my aunt a thousand-dollar bill in an Easter card, no postal insurance or anything. She picked up the phone and called the junkman, had the wringer washer taken to the dump. Grabbed the catalogue and ordered the top-of-the-line washer and dryer. Neighbours who saw her in the backyard, standing on a kitchen chair to pull down the clothesline, balling it up and throwing it over the hill into the ravine, thought she was crazy. My mother put up no fight when I told her I wanted to go out, give it a try for summer work. I think I was getting in her hair anyway, she was looking forward to reaching the empty-nest phase of life. I was going into grade twelve that fall, hoping to get into the dental hygiene course. Who ever thought I'd end up in banking? Well, I said I'd just go the one summer, be back in the fall for school. My parents paid for my ticket and my aunt called Carl, who said I could stay with him for the summer. My parents were happy I'd be staying with a relative. They probably figured Carl would keep an eye on me or something, that's how naive my parents were. As it turned out, there were two girls from my home town living near Carl and they said I could room with them. I called my mother and told her Carl was living the wild life, told her I was planning to knit some chunky wool sweaters on circular needles. Things worked out better that way because for the first while all I did was clean up after Carl who was as messy as a p-i-g, thinking you only had to do the dishes once a week, only wash your clothes if there was nothing clean left in the closet.

It took me some time to adjust to the place, the way the sun just never seemed to go down. Lots of apartments had aluminum foil stuck over the bedroom windows. It looked funny, a big high-rise in the middle of nowhere, scraggy bog all around, no trees, and half the windows in the place all silver and shiny.

The heat and the bugs took some getting used to. The apartment building I stayed in with the girls had a sauna and a little pool on the main level. The girls and I used the sauna a lot, mostly because the air outside felt cooler after a session in the heat. Plus we used to sit there and gossip about men.

You couldn't walk down the street without every second truck or car honking at you, guys leaning out to whistle and catcall, proposing marriage or something worse. Well, looking back, marriage was worse. Oprah should have done a show on that place, about what it could do for a woman's self-esteem. A combination of factors made the town so wild — partly it was boys who'd never had twenty bucks in their wallets getting overtime paycheques for three grand, taking them to the bank and asking for the cash. We were all from away. I only ever met one local person, the guy who owned the drugstore. So, like I was saying, you take these boys and give them lots of cash, take away the rain and the night and put them with a bunch of their buddies, little wonder they were wild for women.

One thing I loved about those fellows is how they'd always see a woman's best feature. Take Prudence, one of the girls I roomed with. Now Prudence had a small bust, always used to be self-conscious about it at home. In high school, guys would pass her mean notes; "Chalk-board flat, fried eggs, the rain'll always hit your feet, not worth the effort to feel you up." She used to wear big sweatshirts, even in the heat of the summer. By the time I got to McMurray, Prudence was out of her shell. She'd walk right down the main drag in a little tube top and shorts; twice she caused a car to rear-end the guy in front. You see, Prudence had great legs and when we sat in the sauna she used to tell us what the guys said, all of them singing her praises, not one of them saying he wished she had bigger tits. People can really shine if you throw a little light on their strong points.

Getting back to the main story, Oprah and my friend Bonnie. Well, if I was to run into an old boyfriend every up and coming Friday, I'd be at it for a while. The thing is, for all those nice young men from my summer in McMurray, I only fell in love once. One time. And wouldn't it be some-one whose name I kept choking on? His name was Graham, which I kept wanting to pronounce like gram of hash. His friends called him "Gray-ham", like there was a "y" in it some-where. I used to have to concentrate every time I said it. You'd think a girl would naturally love the name of the man she loved, but not me. All I wished was that he'd change it or get a nickname or something.

If you didn't know the whole story, this next bit would be embarrassing. You see, Graham was a nurse. The reason he was a nurse, though, was that he was applying to medical school and figured it would help him be a better doctor if he first had a nurse's perspective. I could hardly believe it when he told me. The night we met I was working at the Pier Eight, waitressing. Gives you some idea how many Maritimers were living there, they go and call a place in the middle of the prairies Pier Eight — never mind the only scent of the sea out there was the odd whiff of Old Spice. It was a big restaurant with a bar attached. For fifteen bucks you got a meal — two things to choose from, filet mignon or chicken cordon bleu, plus a drink and dessert. Thursday through Saturday we had live entertainers. Valdy even came once. We had an Elvis impersonator who did a fine job of "Suspicious Minds". Anyway, Graham ended up coming to the restaurant with three other nurses, on account of one of them was leaving because her husband had got transferred to Seattle. I had their table to wait. They were a nice bunch, ended up tipping me twenty bucks. I admit I was putting the moves on Graham, as much as I could considering I had six other tables. We were talking about desserts and it turned out my favourite dessert was the same as his, poppyseed cake. He told me he was from Toronto and a little bit about applying to medicine. I told him about the dental hygienist thing, in truth I made it sound like I was already in the program. Sometimes something happens, call it fate, call it whatever you want, but the thing turns out to be a piece of real magic in an otherwise ordinary life.

The next night, when I got to work to start my shift, Mrs. Wong, my boss, told me someone had been in earlier and left a parcel. It was a poppyseed cake, baked by Graham with a note: "Enjoy your favourite. Don't forget to floss. From Graham". He didn't put his phone number on the card but I called him at the hospital the next day. A lot of our shifts conflicted but we finally managed to meet one night after he finished work at eight. We went to a piano bar on top of a hotel and had a drink. No one ever asked to see your ID in that place, never. I had a Bloody Caesar and he had a scotch. Is it too late to tell you he looked like a cross between Ringo Starr and Gino Vannelli? Graham and I no shortage of things to talk about that night. In fact, we stayed at the bar until it closed and then he walked me home. We held hands. Understand that I was fully anticipating going to bed with him at once, immediately. We got to the foyer of my building and he sat on the bench beside the artificial palm tree. I sat beside him and then he told me he was engaged to a girl back in Toronto. He even pulled out his wallet and showed me her picture, and of course I hated her immediately, hated her stupid picture. She had a bad perm and beady eyes, shark eyes, like in *Jaws*. Oh, and of course her name, Isabelle. Sounded like a romance novel or the kind of girl in those detective magazines my cousin Carl had at his place, big black rectangles covering the girl's faces. I asked him why he'd made me the cake and he said because he wasn't sure how he felt about getting married, that he was "uncertain of the future". I vowed then and there to spend the next three weeks convincing him to dump old Isabelle. I even pictured us living in Toronto, right down to how the street would look, which was absurd given I had never been to Toronto.

The weeks passed quickly, but not before I fell further in love with Graham. He told me up front that we couldn't sleep together, that we couldn't do anything of that nature at all, so I agreed, embarked on a period of no sex. If you think that wasn't hard, what with the whole town doing it day and night, let me tell you this — yes it was hard, but no it wasn't either, because I was in love. One night I even sat on his couch and watched the rest of a movie alone while he talked to Isabelle on the phone, which was a torture like you cannot imagine. Finally the summer was over. He said he'd drive me to the airport. Gave me a card and said not to open it until I was on the plane. He kissed me for the first time, probably the sweetest kiss of my life except I was crying by then. The card said pretty much what I expected. That he would be getting married, about his family and her family and commitment and all that. Then it went on to say that although he felt he shouldn't tell me, that he had nothing to offer and intended never to see me again, he did love me in a way he'd never loved anyone else. Not even Isabelle. But still that didn't mean he could let all those people down. I suppose I could have called him when I got back to the Maritimes, argued my case, but I didn't know his number. Besides, what would I have said?

Worked real hard that fall but my marks still weren't good enough to get into dental hygiene. Ended up at community college for six months and then at the bank. For two years I dated Vern, a fishing maniac. Then I got a chance for a job transfer to Calgary, in the chequing department of the bank. I said yes straight off. And I'm still here, land of milk and honey as they say. I met and married Gordon, another Maritimer, faster than you can use up a line of credit, poof. Had my babies that quick too, partly because I wanted to get on with my life, partly because Gordon is older than me. I've always kind of looked older, good but older, mind you. My girls are now entering the teenaged years, thinking of boys all the time. It was that stupid Oprah show put Graham back in my mind.

I'm thinking I might go pay my phone bill at the phone company. I hear they have all the different phone books for every province there. I think I'll just look at the Toronto listings, or maybe in the Yellow Pages under "Physicians". I suppose if his name is there I could write to him. Maybe he didn't get married. Maybe he's miserable. Oprah said not to do it. Said you should look inside yourself and work out the unresolved rejection. When I look inside myself — well hell, who has time to do that, with work and family and all? It's not so much that I'm lonely, either. I don't know what it is. Wanting to tie up loose ends or something. Gordon wants us to move back east. My parents would love it, so would his mother. I guess that's it, a spring-cleaning feeling, just wanting to sort out any unfinished business from this province. I would just like to hear his voice one more time.

REM SLEEP

A week after I had my tubes cut, my husband dreamed I grew a penis. Well, I haven't grown a penis but over the years I have grown to expect just this sort of thing from Gordon. He told me the dream as soon as he awoke, sitting on the side of the bed, scratching his ear. Every morning is the same — he tells of his dreams while I lay listening, watching the sun lick the spiders' webs in the corners of the bedroom ceiling. His dreams often feature his new truck. Sometimes he dreams he's driving but it's like a Fred Flintstone car and he has to walk his feet along the road to keep it moving. He keeps coming to hills to go up but none to go down. Sometimes he dreams of his dead father. In these dreams Gordon comes up to him and whispers, "Aren't you supposed to be dead?" and his father puts his fingers to his lips, then smiles and says, "Shhhhh. Don't tell on me now, boy," and they laugh.

The operation was my idea. I knew Gordon wasn't keen on the whole thing but I was fed up with the diaphragm, all that jelly smearing everywhere, searching for it in the cold morning bathroom and it bouncing back into shape outside my body. I was tired of washing and drying it, holding it up to the light, looking for that possible tiny pinhole that could change my fate for ever. My two daughters, Claire and Rebecca, are fine, plenty for me. Plus they're getting older now and I never planned on trying for a boy, ending up with three or maybe even four girls, no thank you. I'm the sort of person who plans my life and takes charge. I don't just let life happen to me.

The world is made up of two kinds of people, and it's easy to tell them apart during winter. The first kind you'll know because their car windows are clear when they drive down the road. The mornings with heavy frost and ice, they go out ten minutes early and start the car, turning the defrost on high and pushing the heat lever all the way to the red end. Then they go back inside for a bit. When they come out again, they use a scraper, not a credit card or an empty cassette case. They have a real scraper from Canadian Tire that does the job well. After the front window is clean they scrape the side windows and always the rear window. Be sure to look for the rear windows being done, because people that just do the front fall into the next category. Finally, they get in the car and drive off, the engine down to its normal humming. You can bet that these people have a bag of sand in the trunk, at the very least, and that their windshield-washer fluid isn't going to run out. I mean, if you can't see the guy's face through his salt-smeared window, you can be sure he's not getting a good picture of you.

The second group of people run out to the car on those finger numbing days, start the engine, leap out to scrape a hole on the front windshield large enough for a small cat to crawl through, jump in and drive off. They probably have a cup of coffee in one of those plastic sipper mugs from Tim Horton's stuck on the dash, and the steam from it will melt another telltale small hole in the frost on the windshield. They can feel the stiffness as they force the gearshift into first and drive off, engine still racing, but let me tell you, that's the least of their worries. It's as easy as that to tell who's who and what the rest of their life is like, and how they think, or rather don't. And it's not just lazy — it's selfish.

I made an appointment with my doctor, Dr. Plaxton. He delivered the girls. He thought I was sensible and said there was nothing to it, just in through the belly-button, snip, snip. His nurse called later with a surgery date. Gordon drove me both ways because it was day surgery.

I felt happy and relieved, coming to in recovery. It felt like the end of a chapter, a good chapter with a neat end. I hate books that leave you hanging in the air, wondering what happened. I knew Gordon was sad about the whole thing. He doesn't like endings, neat or otherwise. He didn't try to talk me out of it, but when I told him I was going to have it done he just sat at the kitchen table, turning his coffee mug around and around. Having kids mellowed him out a lot. He had a sad little smile that could break your heart if you're that kind of person, but I'm not. I got up and kissed his forehead and brought the plates to soak in the sink so the egg wouldn't stick on them.

Gordon was slow in getting the penis dream told. I'm always patient and I listen carefully. Sometimes I ask questions at the end. His dream didn't surprise me. I guess he saw the operation as making me less of a woman — not quite a man, but less of a woman all the same. I asked him what he thought of me having a penis and he said he was kind of interested, seeing as how it was still really me. Then he said I wasn't very friendly about the whole thing, didn't seem to welcome his messing with me, so he stopped and that was the end. I rolled towards him and rubbed his back. He gave a little snorting laugh and got up to wash and shave.

A month later he bought me a puppy, asked if I was surprised, and I lied and said yes. It was my birthday. The year before, he gave me a leather jacket. The year before that, he gave me an opal ring because opal is my birthstone. We always exchange gifts for our anniversary too, and on Valentine's Day I get flowers. He knows that sort of thing is important to me. My oldest daughter, Claire, named the dog Rose. A nice dog, looks like a cross between a beagle and a terrier, kind of mixed brown and black wiry fur.

I joined obedience classes. My friend Bonnie from back home wrote and told me dogs need to be started young if they're going to be well trained. She has a standard poodle, because of her allergies and all. The class meets once a week in the United Church hall. The instructor is a woman — tough, but I like her. She puts long strips of black rubberized floor runner in a big square and we stand on that, spread out to give each other room.

There are ten dogs in the class, "First-Level Family Companion". If a dog messes it's no problem — there's a can of Lysol spray, paper towels and a pile of empty plastic grocery bags. The first thing we learned was how to pick up a dog mess, with our hand protected by the bag, and tie it shut to throw it out. Then we learned how to stop the dogs from barking by looking them in the eye, holding their mouths closed, and saying in a firm voice, "No bark." This works well for all the dogs except one, Raven is her name. I'm not sure what kind of dog she is, very tiny, long silky fur. Her owner seems a little flaky. You wouldn't think such a small dog would make such a racket but she does, that yapping that just makes your hair stand on end. The instructor makes Raven's owner throw a towel over her — this is the next step if the "no bark" doesn't work. Try to imagine how funny it looks to see a little hump under a pink bath towel, moving around and around, still barking but the sound muffled by the towel.

Rose is a model student. We get handouts that talk about dog behaviour, how dogs go through adolescence just like kids do, test the rules, fall into bad behaviour. Not Rose, though. After a week of training she never messed in the house any more and, thank God, she has never been a dog that barks, from the day we got her.

Jeremy is the name of the fellow who stands next to me. The instructor makes us stand in a certain order because some of the dogs are too high-strung to be next to certain other dogs. I'd say Jeremy is about thirty, skinny as a rake. His dog, Chester, is a German shepherd. The thing's as crazy as a bag of hammers — bites at invisible flies and hides his face between his paws when he's in the down position — but Jeremy just laughs. He's the produce manager at the grocery store. I must have noticed him before, spraying the lettuce or something.

Chester and Rose got their leads tangled leaving the hall last night. Everyone else had gone. The instructor was in the basement, getting the vacuum to clean up stray dog hairs. Rose just sat down; she has such a quiet temperament. Chester stood there stupidly, tongue hanging out, grinning with black gums. I bent over to get the leads straightened and when I stood my hair had fallen across my face. Gentle as you please, Jeremy reached over and pushed my hair back, cupped my cheek in his hand and smiled. It all happened in a matter of seconds. Then he left, Chester pulling ahead on the lead making choking sounds like some dogs do, and me standing in the doorway, staring after them.

When I got home Gordon was watching television, a boxing match. The girls were at a friend's house for a sleep-over. I decided to have a bath so I put Rose in her cage and got my robe and slippers, headed for the bathroom. Baths always make me sleepy. By the time I got out and went to the bedroom, Gordon was asleep, so I crawled in beside him, turned out my bedside lamp and went to sleep.

I dreamed I was at the grocery store with a list about three feet long. I had Rose with me, her lead tied to the cart. Seemed every aisle I went up there were a dozen things I needed from the list, so I'd tell Rose to sit and I'd scoop stuff off the shelves, pile it into the cart. When I got to the produce aisle the whole section of the store looked like a tropical retreat. Palm trees, not in pots but growing straight out of the floor. The weird part was that there were no other shoppers, just me and Rose. Down at the end of produce, near the bags of potatoes, was a waterfall, and Rose started pulling and whining to go there. Just as we reached the falls and I could feel the fine spray on my face and arms, who should show up but Jeremy with his dog, Chester. Jeremy was wearing shorts, a tee-shirt and sunglasses, the mirror kind where you can't see a person's eyes. Chester was loose, not on a lead, so I reached over and unhooked Rose. Then — this part is so strange — didn't the two dogs start to go at it! Mating! You'd think I would have panicked, because Rose isn't fixed, but no, I stood there like it was the most normal thing in the world. Poor Rose looked so small with Chester on her backside. When I was a kid and neighbourhood dogs got together, some adult always showed up with a hose or a bucket of water to throw on them. It never worked, the water, and the dogs stayed locked. Why would anybody think water would get them unstuck? Must have been thinking of cold showers for men, or how wading into the ocean makes a man's penis shrink up. Well anyway, in the dream no one throws water. Jeremy comes over and stands close beside me, takes my hand, and we watch these dogs going at it. I glance at him but I can't see his eyes because of the stupid sunglasses.

Then Gordon nudged me in the side, in real life, and I woke up. It was morning and Rose was crying to go out. I never for one minute considered telling the dream to Gordon. He's quite jealous, though he likes to pretend he's not. See, there had to be something to the dream about me being attracted to Jeremy. That much I understood. Not as if the dream was trying to make me remember to buy bananas and oranges because my kids had eaten all the fresh fruit in the house. I got up, groped my way into my bathrobe and went downstairs. After Rose had run off, I plugged in the kettle and heard Gordon go into the bathroom. I got down the cups and took a dog biscuit from the box on the shelf — Rose still needs to get treats at random intervals to reinforce her training. Then I went to the door to call her.

WHY THE SEA
IS BOILING HOT

Robert stretches, pushing a fist into the ball of stiffness in his lower back, while his wife searches the car for her make-up bag. They have been driving for a little over two hours before stopping at this gas bar and restaurant. Lisa heads for the washroom after they order breakfast — Robert asks for Raisin Bran with skim milk and Lisa requests poached eggs. Most of the other customers are men, workers from the tire plant ten minutes down the road. Occasional bursts of laughter come from the men, a guffawing sound that makes Robert expect to see them clapping each other on the back. What they are talking about he can surmise — the general banter of men, nothing really. Probably one man will be humorous, the others leaning back in the booth seats to let him tell the stories. Maybe he'll tell one they've heard before. Perhaps they fish or hunt together or play on the same softball team. Quite possibly one of them planted maple trees in his yard which porcupines attack each night, turning efforts at landscaping into a heap of toothpicks.

Robert owns a store, Country Hearth, that sells wood-stoves and fireplace inserts. His business venture coincided with the wave of nostalgic country yearnings and unprec-edented spending of young couples in the early 1980s. The store prospers, has had two expansions and retains all but one of the original staff, men who tell people what a great place it is to work.

When Lisa returns from the washroom she frowns at the sounds of laughter, as if the workers, new to the day, were already sweaty and stained with grease. Robert feels the tug of nerve under his left eye, a twitch that started four years ago when his father died of liver cancer, turned as yellow as a dirty schoolbus. The twitch has never fully left him but hav-ing observed himself in a bathroom mirror once, twitching like mad, he realizes that the movement is nearly invisible to observers. Still, it feels as if his eyelid is being yanked vio-lently to the left.

Two nights earlier at a Ramada Inn on the outskirts of Calgary, Robert spent the night sitting at the desk in their room, eating pistachio nuts and making preliminary sketches of a shed. They had visited Lisa's brother, Gordon, and his wife, Wanda Lee, for the afternoon. That was as long as Lisa could stand to be around Wanda Lee. Gordon showed Robert a new shed they'd had built and Robert begin to think of building one when they got back to B.C. The shed started out eight feet by ten, then grew to ten by twelve as he drew, trying to make room for the garden tools and also leave stor-age for two cords of hardwood. He has never slept well, in fact can't recall the last time he had a sound sleep.

If asked, he would say he doesn't dream, not at all. He has told several people this over the years, all of whom responded with various shades of incredulity. Most of them tried to make him believe otherwise. *Of course you have dreams — you just don't remember them. Everybody dreams. Why, I read somewhere that if you didn't dream you'd go crazy.* His wife says he's lying, that he has dreams but won't talk about them. Accustomed as she is to his nocturnal roaming, she sleeps soundly, dreams frequently and never stirs as he passes the hours of night.

The trip was the suggestion of their marriage therapist, Beryl Ludley, a woman who spends most of her professional time concentrating on a new breathing technique she's learning from a home-study course on visualization.

"He's so quiet. Last time the two of us talked, I mean what you'd actually call a half-decent conversation … God, I can't even remember when that was."

Based on what Lisa said and the willingness with which Robert paid the substantial bills of the therapy clinic, Beryl Ludley felt a holiday might be just the thing. She even recommended the location, Jasper National Park, for two reasons. Her L. L. Bean catalogue had come in the morning mail and she'd flipped the pages in the washroom stall, decided to order plaid flannel sheets and a log-cabin quilt for her bed. This had set her thinking of rustic settings, mountain lodges and coffee in blue speckled mugs, things far away from the city. Then her accountant had called with good news on her mutual holdings, which had caused her to consider interest accrued, the uncomplicated joy of spending money. These occurrences merged in a flash that prompted her to suggest a trip to Robert and Lisa not an hour later.

"It's a lot of driving," Robert argued.

"I like the idea," Lisa countered.

"Don't let compromise be such a sour taste to you, Robert," Beryl said. "Happiness takes on many ever-changing forms. You have to be prepared to adapt to its demands."

While Robert pays for breakfast, Lisa, convinced she's left her allergy nose spray at the motel, selects a cold remedy from the slim selection of medicines behind the counter. Although at first he believes the thought unkind, he feels pleased when the pill causes her to fall asleep an hour later. Traffic is light and he begins to enjoy driving; his shoulders drop and he rubs the back of his neck with one hand. To know he won't be dragged or cajoled into conversation fills him with fluid relief. Both of them would agree that all they do now is fight — never mind if the conversation starts out innocently enough — and if they aren't actually fighting, they are trying to use the new communication methods Beryl is teaching them. Lisa calls this their pretend talking.

Her brother Dan called last month and asked for money. She wired him five-hundred dollars. That same night the phone rang again and Robert answered.

"Hi Bob."

"Oh, hi, Gordon. Lisa's not home right now."

"That's okay. Listen, just tell her not to send Danny any money. I sent him a grand today. Tell her … tell her I was talking to Mom and he's okay but just not to send any more money."

When Lisa got home and Robert gave her the message, she accused him of interfering with her family life.

"I'm your family."

"No, you're my husband. Danny is my family. You keep out of it."

Robert knew early in the marriage that he couldn't make any suggestions to Lisa, that if he did she would misconstrue his helpfulness as commands or orders.

"Don't ever tell me what to do," she said to him.

One time she talked about an old boyfriend, she didn't give a lot of details, but Robert was left wondering if Lisa had chosen him for his quietness and then grown to resent that characteristic.

While Lisa sleeps and he drives, he is able to watch her undisturbed. This is something he often does at home, propped on his elbow in their bed. She has both an abandon and a peacefulness in sleep that makes him wish she would never move again, or rather, that she would awaken and retain the serenity of her sleep. From what he's seen on a television show about sleep, he would expect her to curl into a fetal ball, pulling knees to chest, blankets twisted round like a hamster in a cocoon of shredded tissue. But no, her arms are often above her head, curved, fingers held apart as if cupping a butterfly.

Lisa works in hospital administration. She has had three miscarriages. The first time she was relieved. She and Robert had just started sleeping together, weren't talking future plans or marriage. She missed her period but told no one, waited and six weeks later miscarried. Over the next five years she lost two more pregnancies. Her doctor told her to keep trying, to think of these events as little setbacks. Then she began staring at pregnant women and thinking they looked exhausted, stretched and swollen, veins bulging on their legs. *Perhaps she wasn't missing anything* was what she began to think. *Perhaps it was a conspiracy, misery enjoys company, a silent agreement to lure all women into the trap of being tired and irritated and just plain used up.* She and Robert discussed adoption, but that was as far as it went, discussion. Robert was afraid to push the issue any further and Lisa did nothing to move the idea towards reality.

There is no need for her to work, and they treat her salary as disposable income. Mostly they use it for travel. The last trip they took was to England, where they rented a houseboat on the Norfolk Broads for a week. Then two days in London, and the last three days in a bed-and-breakfast in Colchester, a three-storey brick house with a goldfish pond in the backyard. Their room was small, the bed soft.

Lisa slept poorly in that bed, was irritable during the visit to the zoo. They drove to a pub for lunch, decided to sit at the outdoor tables, and it was at that moment that she felt love slip, like a sand castle falling apart — first one grain, then a turret sliding sideways, collapsing an archway. Confused and perhaps frightened, she was fairly certain that nothing was her fault.

"You've changed," she said.

"What?"

"You've changed. I hadn't noticed it until now but you have."

"How do you mean?"

"Just you're not the same."

Robert hadn't changed one bit, in fact hasn't changed since he was twenty-four. He was in the shower of the university dormitory and started crying, surprising himself, and couldn't stop. He let himself cry for a long time, so long his chest hurt afterwards. The moment was one of facing his grief and loneliness, confronting the enormity of what appeared before him as a lifetime of isolation, impenetrable. His roommate, a Dutch exchange student taking the same business degree, commented on Robert's mood at that time, which gave him a degree of comfort. He told Robert that there was a Dutch phrase for it but that the translation was difficult; loosely it meant "he now fit his own skin".

Sitting at the patio table in the pub garden, Lisa looked at Robert and felt her field of vision shatter, as if an errant baseball had flown unintentionally through a picture window. What she had initially perceived as his pensiveness had become a void of thoughtlessness. The charm of his patience smelled of boredom. She felt angry and alone, duped, cemented to the wrought-iron chair beneath the mocking summer sun.

Robert never had a chance to find out what truly happened in that moment — not that he could have, not that these things can ever be spoken. A room full of words — the truth, the influence of the past — might as well be empty for all the good it could do. Beryl Ludley believes she knows the answers, believes she sees the big picture. Sometimes she gets so frustrated with clients. She thinks most of them are afraid of the truth, that a look at bone-bare reality would have them screaming and falling apart. She hates being a therapist — wanted to do graphic design but the job prospects in that field were slim.

Starting in Colchester, Lisa became an emotional pursuer — that's what Beryl calls her. Beryl says Robert distances himself, an emotional retreater.

Their fights are largely one-sided, begin with Lisa becoming angry over not Robert's actions but rather his inaction, what she sees as indecision. There is name-calling on her part, some pleading, condemnation and ultimately tears. He left once, while she was still sitting on the couch, twisting a throw pillow into a ball. She opened the window as he walked down the driveway to the car.

"You goddamned coward. Don't bother coming back."

Of course he came back, where else was there to go? After that episode they started working with Beryl.

A pothole awakens Lisa and she straightens her legs, puts on sunglasses.

"Do you want a coffee?" she asks.

"Do you?"

"That's what I just asked you, Bob. Do YOU want a coffee?"

"Sure. I'll look for a place to stop."

"Do you want coffee or are you just saying that? I think you only say what you think I want to hear."

He doesn't say anything, but passes two tractor trailers and pulls up close behind a large truck with an antiquated canvas covering. The sunbleached covering stretches over steel arches and reminds Robert of an aged circus ride, somewhat ludicrous. He can smell cows, he thinks, the odour of fields and manure, and switches the air vents to recirculate. Morning traffic has increased and there is little room to manoeuvre, no opportunity to overtake.

"I don't think I love you any more," Lisa says, watching the line of trees fly backwards in the side mirror of the car.

Robert knows he will leave her when the trip is over. He can envision going to the grocery store and asking for boxes to pack his things. No more fighting, he thinks. He wonders if Lisa will be happy when he is gone, if she'll laugh or maybe even fall in love. He can't wait to be alone, all alone. He is not concentrating on his driving and comes too close to the truck in front of him, comes so close that he must brake sharply.

A pig's head pushes against the canvas, near a rotting seam that gives way, tearing the weakened cloth in a long straight line. The head is huge, ears larger than dinner plates and very upright. Robert thinks the edge of them looks as thick as his thumb. The cartoon-like snout looks predictable, upturned, nostrils flecked with bits of hay or grass. The eyes seem small in comparison to the head, not particularly bright, certainly not the eyes of a wise or even frightened pig. Robert starts to brake gently; the distance between the two vehicles grows to three car-lengths, five, seven. The pig still appears enormous, and as Robert glances down to check his speed, the pig jumps. He watches it land on the highway, roll over about ten times. It doesn't appear hurt. When it reaches the gravel shoulder, it rights itself and heads towards the mountains in the distance. Gripping the steering wheel less tightly, Robert half-turns to watch the pig, until a crest in a hill causes him to lose sight of it.

LAST DANCE

"You were a real bitch."

Those words were my first clue to his anger. If there were other indications, I'd missed them. Visual clues: the tightness in his jaw; a vacancy in his eyes, as if he was afraid to give something away. It's understandable I missed the signs, someone I hadn't seen for twenty years. And not to be cruel, but pretty much a nobody all those years ago.

I've worn glasses since fourth grade and I believe the evidence that, when one sense is damaged, the others compensate for the loss. That's how it's been with my hearing — the worse my eyes got, the keener my ears.

My sixth sense, my intuition, also serves me well — I'm a wise but reticent critic and an invaluably sympathetic ear for a deserving few. I don't smoke. I quit twelve years ago when one of my friends — an old teacher actually, Mr. Garrod — died of lung cancer. I only drink socially, which for me is about six times a year — Christmas, New Year's, birthdays and weddings.

A wedding is what brought me back to this hole. It still amazes me that my brother and his family moved back here. Homesick was the reason, they said. Sick, I'd say. I wish I could think of one nice thing to say about this city but I can't. Beat it out of here as soon as I could save the money after high school graduation, and succeeded in putting the distance I wanted between this place and me — the whole country. I live on the west coast now; send my mother money every Christmas so she can purchase a ticket and visit me for three weeks in the spring. Real spring, not what passes for spring in the Maritimes — ice pellets beating down the few daffodils that manage to surface through the mud. My mother has visited every year since my father died. I didn't come home for the funeral, couldn't see the point.

I'm not entirely sure why I agreed to come home for the wedding — I kept hoping they'd elope or something. My niece Claire phoned to invite me, her Sunday-morning call ringing me awake at seven-thirty.

"Yes?"

"Auntie Lisa! You were asleep, weren't you!"

Claire loves to declare the obvious, she always has. I remember her standing in the sandbox once, laughing, a puddle staining the powdery sand, yelling, "I'm peeing. I'm peeing now!"

Claire is my favourite niece and I tell my brother Gordon that I got the best of the deal — all the fun of her and none of the worry. That's a lie, though. *I did worry* — it's my nature. The bumps and scrapes, the first piano recital, which I flew to Calgary for, my fingers kneading the damp program in my lap, willing her to remember the notes. Her first date and now marriage; a good match, all told. He's prone to a bit of ruminating, but Claire will yell him back into the real world whenever she needs to. They spent a week with me last summer at the end of their cross-country bicycle tour, a misnomer if ever I heard one. My brother's money kept them well fed, with hotel room service and plane tickets here, there and everywhere. The bikes spent most of the holiday locked up in storage closets of hotel lobbies, wrapped in the blurry plastic of giant Air Canada baggies.

Don't get me wrong, I'm glad that my brother's generous. He's a good father to both Claire and Rebecca, a good man, kind. That's the real reason I keep in touch, loner that I am.

"Dad says he'll fly you home for the wedding," Claire squealed into the phone. "Isn't that great!"

"Give me the dates again, Claire," I said, fumbling for my glasses on the cluttered bedside table. I found them, grabbed the pen beside my journal and flipped it open to an empty page.

"The wedding is on Saturday the fourth, but Dad says he wants you to come on Wednesday if you can and leave whenever. Just book it and fax him the stuff."

Claire gains both momentum and volume in all her conversations. I was fully awake by then and needing the bathroom.

"Tell him I'll book it tomorrow. I have to go now but I'll see you soon," I said, trying to match her fervour but knowing I sounded cagey, anxious to get her off the phone. "I love you, honey, bye for now."

I put down the receiver and hurried towards the bathroom, still naked. I sleep naked, summer and winter. For summer I use a light duvet but I own an Arctic-grade one too, not that it ever gets that cold. It pays to be prepared, especially living alone. I've been divorced for three years now.

After I peed, I brushed my teeth and smiled at myself in the bathroom mirror. It's funny to see my body now, the changes. There's a good hint of what's to come, but in my mind, in my mind I sometimes feel exactly like I did when I was eighteen. Oh sure, there's a sense of "if I knew then what I know now ..." It's hard to describe but I look at this woman of forty and I see the young girl, tanned and lean and horny, well yes, *horny*. Not that I really see her, but I do know her, as she was twenty-two years ago. Eighteen. By then I had already screwed a healthy portion of eligible men in the port city. I started at sixteen. To me, virginity was a nuisance, a zit to be popped, got rid of. Once it was gone, I set about to satisfy my curiosity. Oh, I was careful and choosy, though, and escaped getting a bad reputation. People who've only been with one or two partners can't imagine just how interesting it is — to see someone and wonder how they look naked, how they kiss, how they make love, and then actually find out. Kind of like being allowed to taste a whole box of mixed chocolates after someone threw out the identification sheet. Well, finding out is revealing, to say the least. It's an education in more ways than you'd ever imagine. I'm not saying it's for everyone but for me, for me it was a necessary thing. And though this may come as a shock, I was never unfaithful in my marriage.

My ageing body ... When I was in my early twenties, I read an awful article in *Cosmopolitan* and stood in front of a mirror, smug when the pencil placed beneath my naked breast fell to the floor with a congratulatory smack. "The perfect breast will not hold a pencil beneath it and should fit into a champagne glass." Ha, these days I'm sure I could hold up a bottle of beer and I'd fit a Tupperware container suited for leftovers, but I don't give a damn. Funny, the further I get from so-called perfection, the greater my love for my body.

Now Bob, my ex-husband, has this obsession with fitness — it really took over after we divorced — a terror of cholesterol. He used to urge me to come for those six a.m. jogs. High-fibre Bob. No, I don't miss him. I picture him in the future, frantically running from death just as long as he can still put one foot in front of the other, maybe even forcing a walker in front of him near the end. Poor Bob.

Now I'm relaxed. I eat when I please, what I please. I tidy up when I want to, read as late as I like. I usually get a gelato after work and eat it perched on a high wooden stool in the deli, reading the newspaper.

There is this man, of sorts, in my life now. A paper man … ha ha, like those ones I had as a kid that you could dress up in paper clothes with tabs on the back. I found him in the personal ads, which I have always read out of interest. What's sad is how boring most of them are, uninteresting and so much the same, but every so often there's a great one, so reading them is worthwhile. Of course it was never my intention to actually answer an ad, Jesus no. But I did. From the *Globe and Mail*. I keep it in my purse, actually. It goes:

> Like everyone in these ads, I'm a discerning, attractive, cultured, highly successful, fit, funny, erudite, blah, blah, blah. What it all comes down to though is I'm a forty-two-year-old man. I believe in saving the last dance, composting, that it was a lone assassin, doing the NY Times crossword, getting up early to fish and indulging one's passions.

Now isn't that great? It was the *blah, blah, blah* caused me to write. Then he wrote and I wrote, and he wrote and I wrote. Four months now. He's a wonderful writer. Words mean a lot — a whole lot — to me, so there you have it. I would say the recent letters have an air of sexual tension to them that I find exhilarating. Anyone else reading them would say, "Tension? Where? Sexual? Are you nuts?" But it's there, woven in ever so subtly. He knows that I'm going to the east coast for a wedding and that I have a two-day stop-over in Toronto on the way back. And yes, we're getting together.

Flying bothers my ears. I hold my nose with my fingers and blow, trying to force my Eustachian tubes open as the plane taxis to a stop along the runway. We have to walk on the tarmac to get to the terminal — primitive or what? I expect to see a volunteer fire department passing the baggage hand to hand from the plane to the conveyor belt beside the building. You can be sure no one in this neck of the woods would get credit for inventing the wheel. It's that sort of place, "timeless" but not like they mean in the travel brochures. No, that's not completely true. A few years ago they demolished a whole row of two-hundred-year-old buildings, the stone gargoyles bludgeoned to dust under the wrecking balls, all to make way for a mall of chain stores that went bankrupt the next year. No, it's not fair to say nothing changes — it does, but never for the better. There is no reverence here.

The wedding goes off without a hitch. Claire is divine, quiet for once, three thousand dollars worth of orthodontic efforts gleaming in the opulent June sun. My brother struts in the background. Success agrees with him; it always has, and he attracts it. Wanda Lee looks like a psycho version of an old beauty queen, the kind you see waving from a float in a parade, surrounded by tissue-paper carnations. She must have bought the dress here, turquoise — it's wild. Mother of the bride. My other brother, Dan, is in detox for his third round. The past few years have been really rough for him. He probably wouldn't have come to this anyway, though.

I take a lot of photos, not because I like pictures but because the camera fends off guests who might want to chat. I spend a lot of time focusing and eventually the crowd begins to thin. The bride and groom disappear. They're going to Jamaica for three weeks, this time without the bikes.

I feel someone bump my chair and I look up. He's tall, a little heavy, dark hair and a navy suit.

"Would you like to dance?" he asks.

I have no excuse, there's no one left to photograph. There are only a few die-hard dancers left, the band slugging out a waltz tune, anxious to pack up and leave for the night. He's a good dancer.

"You don't remember me, do you?" he says, grinning.

I lean my head back and peer at him, willing myself to place the face, but it's no use. Couldn't tell him from Adam.

"No, I'm sorry," I say.

"It's Don. Don Maxwell, Wendy's brother."

Wendy, one of my few friends from high school. Her brother came to our graduation party at her family's summer house. Was he one year younger than us or two? I was drunk, without a date, and he and I ended up necking on a musty couch on the veranda, flicking away the ravenous blackflies. Any exposed flesh was fair game for the bugs at that time of year. It was me who pulled him into the empty back bedroom.

I remember standing naked while Wendy's brother cried soundlessly, sitting on the camp cot. I guess he must have still been a virgin. I can barely remember but either he came the second we got our clothes off or he simply went limp. I was quite drunk, but I recall slipping back into my shorts and tee-shirt and leaving the room. I think I told him it didn't matter.

"Bitch."

To call me that is the worst thing someone could say. I know I'm thoughtless at times, less so now than before, but I am not cruel and I have never felt malice. Bitches connive, knowingly wound. This does not apply to me.

As the band grinds to the end of the song, he pulls me close to him, pressing himself against my thigh. The hand holding mine tightens, tightens. He hisses the word in my face again — "Bitch" — in a rush of whisky breath. Then he lets go and walks away.

I stumble to the washroom, lock myself in a stall and lean against the cold metal door. I want to cry but I just can't. Tearing off a piece of toilet paper, I blow my nose and with a brief pain my ears pop and clear. Flushing the wad of toilet paper, I come out and stand at the row of sinks. I open my purse, get a brush and pull my hair back, fasten it with a clasp. Wash my hands. Check my purse and see the return ticket with the Toronto stop-over. Take one more quick glance in the mirror. Meet my eyes, the same for all the years gone by. I reach out and touch the mirror, am shocked by how cold it feels. When I come out of the bathroom, the only people left are the hotel staff, cleaning up.

I bypass the waiting line of taxis outside the hotel and start to walk up King Street. All the stores I remember are gone. I walk towards King Square, thinking I will get a bag of popcorn and feed the pigeons. I can just make them out, grey birds huddled on the bandstand roof.

Pamela Donoghue is a full-time
writer and part-time pharmacist.
She lives with her husband and two
children in Seabright, Nova Scotia.
Her stories have been published in
The Fiddlehead, *Grain*, *The
Antigonish Review*, *Pottersfield
Portfolio*, and the *Maui Review*.
Comfort Zones is her first book.

POLESTAR FIRST FICTION

The First Fiction series celebrates the first published book of fiction — short stories or novel — of a Canadian writer. Polestar is committed to supporting new writers, and contributing to North America's dynamic and diverse cultural fabric.

Polestar Book Publishers takes pride in creating books that enrich our understanding and enjoyment of the world, and in introducing discriminating readers to exciting new writers. Whether in prose or poetry, these independent voices illuminate our history, stretch our imaginations, engage our sympathies and evoke the universal through narrations of everyday life.

Polestar titles are available from your local bookseller. For a copy of our complete catalogue — featuring poetry, fiction, fiction for young readers, sports books and provocative non-fiction — please contact us.

POLESTAR BOOK PUBLISHERS
P.O. Box 5238, Station B
Victoria, British Columbia
CANADA   V8R 6N4
http://mypage.direct.ca/p/polestar/